Frances Eleanor Trollope

Among Aliens

A Novel. Vol. 1

Frances Eleanor Trollope

Among Aliens
A Novel. Vol. 1

ISBN/EAN: 9783337045777

Printed in Europe, USA, Canada, Australia, Japan

Cover: Foto ©Andreas Hilbeck / pixelio.de

More available books at **www.hansebooks.com**

AMONG ALIENS

𝕬 𝕹𝖔𝖛𝖊𝖑

BY

FRANCES ELEANOR TROLLOPE

AUTHOR OF
'THAT UNFORTUNATE MARRIAGE,' 'A CHARMING FELLOW,' 'AUNT MARGARET'S
TROUBLE,' ETC.

IN TWO VOLUMES

VOL. I.

LONDON
SPENCER BLACKETT
ST. BRIDE STREET, LUDGATE CIRCUS, E.C.
1890

THIS STORY

IS

𝔄ffectionately 𝔇edicated

TO

M. S. T.

CONTENTS OF VOL. I.

AMONG ALIENS.

CHAPTER I.

I⊤ seemed to have grown dark suddenly. I had had my eyes fixed on the glory of the sunset. The glow of crimson and purple and gold had died away behind the black dome of St. Peter's, and was succeeded by a long streak of orange colour, clear, intense, and solemn. One star glittered steel-bright above it, and the edges of the distant horizon were dim and vaporous. The profoundly

pathetic beauty of those winter sunsets
from the Pincian always moved me like a
poem or a strain of solemn music. Every
common street sound seemed to jar importu-
nately with the serenity of the wondrous
sky and the mournful stillness of the landscape beneath it. I had a feeling that the
world ought to pause in its noisy whirl and
be silent before that sunset. The air seemed
to be vibrating with memories of the awful
past, and that orange streak in the west to
be intense with a mysterious meaning.

I had gazed at it until my eyes were
dazzled, and when I turned them downward
to the earth, I found that it was dark. It
had been raining but an hour ago, and the
pools of water all along the straight line of
the Via Condotti, where the street lamps
glittered in two converging rows, reflected,
here and there, the lingering lights in the

sky, whilst the houses on either hand were in blackest shadow.

'It is late!' I exclaimed to myself, as I drew my shawl closer against the chill evening air. 'I must make haste home, or Lucy will be uneasy.'

'Home' was not far distant. We lived in a street running steeply uphill from the Via Sistina, in a little lodging on the topmost story. That was all the better in Rome, they said; one was out of the malaria. I did not much concern myself with fears of the malaria (though, indeed, for Lucy's sake, it was well to take what precautions we could; Lucy was not so hardy as I), but the topmost story suited us in various ways. In the first place it suited our purses, which were slender. Then we had, from one window of our sitting-room, a glimpse across the housetops of the distant Campagna, and

1—2

nearly an hour more daylight than our neighbours on the lower floors. I climbed quickly up the long steep stairs, and opened our door with my key. Contrary to my expectation there was no light in the room which served us for drawing-room, study, boudoir, and dining-room, all in one. Lucy had not yet come home, then. A few logs smouldered in the open stove, as I had left them, and the lamp stood ready on the table. I struck a light and fastened the shutters, and blew at the smouldering wood until it blazed cheerfully. It made the shabby room look so pleasant and homelike, that I said aloud, although I was quite alone, ' How I wish Lucy would come home and enjoy it !'

Then I sat down to finish a little study in black and white that I had been making from a plaster cast. I had my work all ready laid out on the table before me, and began to draw. In those days I never knew how time went when once I had my pencil in my hand ; and, indeed, it is much the same with me now. I went on working until I was roused by a violent gust of wind which made the windows rattle. Windows rattle easily in Rome, where the panes of glass are generally loosely fixed into the wooden frames, and where woodwork, as a rule, is made in a crazy, clumsy fashion. But this was a really strong blast of wind. I heard it howl and moan as it swept round the corner of our street. Some drops of rain, too, struck against the glass. The thought that Lucy was out in such wild weather, whilst I was warm indoors, made me shudder sympathetically. I looked at my watch, and was startled to find that it marked a quarter-past six o'clock. I had been drawing for more than an hour, and Lucy had not yet returned! She ought to have been at home long ago. The Palazzo Corleoni, where she went to give lessons in English, was down in the more central part of Rome, near the great church of the Gesù. But that was no distance for a good walker with young, active limbs, like Lucy. Besides, she had never been so late before. I was uneasy. It was in vain that I held my crayon firmly and continued to stare at my plaster model. The lines would not come rightly. My head was anxious and preoccupied, and refused to guide my blundering hand. I threw down the bit of black chalk impatiently.

At that moment the crack-voiced bell began to tinkle, and I ran to open the door, and there stood Lucy with her little gauze veil clinging to her face with moisture, and

drops of rain glistening on her cloak. I un-
clasped the cloak from her shoulders as she
stood, and shook it, and then drew her into
the sitting-room.

' What a nice fire you have !' she said in
her fresh, clear voice. ' I'm a little late, am
I not, Catherine ?'

A lump came up into my throat, and I
felt angry at the same time. It hurt me to
find her so easy and unconcerned, and
talking so carelessly of being ' a little late,'
when I had been suffering real pangs of
anxiety about her. Yes ; I had been
frightened ; and I only knew how oppressive the vague thronging fears had been,
when I saw her standing safe before me.

' A little late,' I answered drily ; and bade
her sit down by the fire and unlace her
wet boots at once, whilst I went back to my
drawing. But the pencil would not obey

me even now. I felt the tremor of one
who is suddenly made aware of a horrible
danger escaped. What if Lucy had not
come home safe! The thought made my
heart sick. I conjured up all sorts of catas-
trophes which might have befallen her,
furtively watching her from my place as she
sat in the shine of the fire. Her hair had
got loose, and fell in wavy curly locks on
to one shoulder; and there were raindrops
glistening on its clear soft brown. She had
very pretty hair: hair of that rare kind
which looks picturesque in disorder. Her
cheeks and her delicate little nose were pink
with the cold, and her pretty small hands
were red and numbed, as she sat fumbling
with chill fingers at the damp bootlace. She
seemed almost the same little Lucy who
used to come to me for help in her struggles
with rebellious buttons and complicated

strings, in our nursery-days. And all at once she lifted up her blue eyes with the very same innocent helpless look I remembered in them when she was three years old, and said, ' I'm afraid I can't undo it, Catherine. My fingers are *so* cold.'

I knelt down before her and unfastened the damp boots, and drew them off, and her stockings too, and rubbed her feet with a dry towel.

' Thank you, Catherine dear,' she said ; ' but it is a shame that you should do that. I can manage now by myself.'

Then finding that I went on chafing her cold little feet, without making her any answer, she said timidly : ' You ain't vexed with me about anything are you, Catty dear ?'

' I am vexed with myself for having been so foolish as to be frightened,' said I, speak-

ing very curtly, and keeping my head bent
down.

'Frightened! Why? About me?'

'You are not usually an hour late; and
when one is alone one gets nervous and
fanciful, I suppose.'

'An hour late! Oh, you must be mistaken, Catherine. They did keep me a
little, but not so long as that. It's impossible.'

I held up my watch, and she looked at it
in amazement. 'Oh, my poor Catherine!'
she exclaimed, putting her arms round my
neck, and her soft cheek against mine;
'how sorry I am! I know how frightened
I should be if you did not come home
punctually;—only you are always punctual.'

I kissed her without letting her find out
that there were tears in my eyes. I could not
give any good reason to myself for their

being there. But I had felt an unusual sense of melancholy and apprehension on me all the evening. The very sunset had seemed more intensely sad than usual ; and to me its beauty is always sad. But such waves of emotion, if they cannot be altogether resisted, are best borne in silence. I hold my breath and keep still, and the tide flows over me and passes away.

Lucy brightened up immediately when I kissed her. Her affectionate nature could not endure that there should be a cloud between us. And, indeed, there had never come a cloud that a word could not dispel.

'And did you work late at the studio ?' she asked. 'And was old Signor Sandro very cross ?'

'Yes ; and no.'

'No ? *I* believe he is always cross ! He would frighten me to death. But you have more courage. Oh, how beautifully you are finishing this chalk study!'

And so she chatted on whilst I filled the little tin tea-kettle with water, and set it on the fire to boil, and got the tea-things ready. We allowed ourselves the luxury of tea of an evening. It reminded us of England, and that, perhaps, was the chief reason why I liked it.

'And now, Lucy,' said I, when we were seated at the table, 'now that you are thawed you must tell me what made you so late. It must not happen again, my child. I don't like your being out in the streets so late alone.'

'I am not afraid, Catherine.'

'That is not the whole question.'

'And besides, you often are out by yourself later than this. Don't you remember when I had the sore throat, how you went

all the way to the chemist's close to the
Popolo, and it was nearly ten o'clock, and
you said——'

'That's very different, Lucy.'

'Why?'

'Because——a young girl alone in the
streets might be molested, or at least
annoyed.'

'And what are you, then, Catty? An
old woman? One would think you were
eighty to hear you talk! But, after all,
you are only six years older than I am.'

'Never mind all that now, Lucy. We
will finish that discussion another time. You
have not answered my question as to how it
came to pass that you are so late.'

'Oh, they kept me at the Palazzo Corleoni.
I mean they asked me to stay a little while.'

'I think the Princess ought to know
better. I am sure you well earn your poor

little pay in an hour. It is too bad to ask for more work out of you, Lucy.'

'Oh, it wasn't the Princess. Besides, I don't grudge a little extra time, dear.'

'Not the Princess? Who was it, then?'

'It was Donna Laura and her brother.'

'What had *he* to do with it?'

'Oh, he came in with a copy of a letter that he wanted translated into English, and Donna Laura said would I help her, just to oblige her brother? And I said yes.'

'What was the letter about?'

'Merely a business letter, about sending a horse he has bought—Don Vittorio has bought—from England. I didn't mind doing it at all, Catherine dear.'

I did not like the proceeding at all; and I said so. They were not above asking a favour, these great people, although their supercilious manner was incessantly reminding us that between the noble and princely House of Corleoni and two obscure English girls, who were trying to earn a living, there was a great gulf fixed. Be it so. For my part I felt no yearning to bridge over the gulf, having my own opinion as to which side of it was the preferable one. But I did not approve of these new advances on the part of Donna Laura's brother. I could not help suspecting that he might have managed to get his letter translated without having recourse to his sister's English teacher, had he chosen to do so. I sat thinking, and, I suppose, frowning over my thoughts, for Lucy said, 'I am sorry you are displeased, dear. And you look so stern that I am almost afraid to give you Donna Laura's message.'

'A message for me? More innovations!'

'She sent you her compliments, and

asked if you would be so very kind as to go
to the Palazzo with me next Wednesday to
look at some drawings of hers. And I—I
think she wants you to do some for her.'

'I should like to send word back that
I only work for love or money, and therefore
am obliged to refuse my services to Donna
Laura de' Principi Bastiani-Corleoni.'

'Oh, you wouldn't do that, Catherine?'

'No. But I should enjoy it. However,
I cannot afford such luxuries as that. What
is it all about? Do you know? If so, give
me a full account, Lucy mine.'

'Well—if you won't mind my rambling a
little—because when my head is very full
of different things, they never will come out
exactly in order——'

'No, no. Ramble away, pussy dear.'

Then she told me that there was to be a
grand bazaar or fancy fair, in aid of a pious

institution in which the ladies of the Roman aristocracy were interested. It was to be a very grand bazaar indeed. The Pope approved it, and had promised a silver vase as his contribution, which was to be raffled for. Cardinals and Monsignori smiled benevolently on the project. All the noble ladies —all those, that is to say, whose families held to the ancient *régime*, and were good *Papalini*—were working for it, and nobody who had even looked at the outside of the Quirinal since the year 1870 was to be allowed to have a hand in it on any pretence whatever. Among the chief promoters of it was the Princess Bastiani-Corleoni. She was to hold a stall with her eldest daughter Donna Laura. Donna Laura had some little reputation as an amateur artist, and her contributions to the stock-in-trade were to consist of water-colour sketches, painted

fans and screens, and objects of that sort.
I was wanted to assist in doing some of
these things, and should, of course, be paid
for my work.   The 'of course' was Lucy's.
I did not feel sure that Donna Laura
intended to pay me.   But I was firmly
resolved that I would make no pencil-stroke
without payment.   I mused a little over
the proposition.

'You will come, won't you, Catherine?
For my sake!   It would be so disagreeable
for me to have to tell them that you refused.'

'I will tell you what I'll do, Lucy; I
will consult Signor Sandro, and if he says
"Go," I will go.'

'Signor Sandro is sure to advise you not
to go.   I know he is.'

'Why, pray?'

'Because he's so crabbed and cross.   And
besides, he is a Red Republican, and he was

exiled in the '48, and—and—I *know* he won't let you go.'

I was a little surprised at Lucy's political information. But I let the subject drop then, and our talk drifted away to other things;—drifted to our childish days, as it so often did; to the pretty home in a suburb of a great English town where we had been born and bred; to the time when my father brought home a second wife, Lucy's mother, a gentle, soft creature whom my brother and I were determined to hate before we saw her, and whom we adored and petted and ruled over before she had been a week in the house : to Lucy's self as a tiny blue-eyed baby, with the patientest, most plaintive little face, whom I held in my arms when I was little more than a baby myself. Her mother died when my half-sister was barely a twelvemonth old, and Lucy loved to hear me talk of the sweet, dead mother whom she had no remembrance of. And now our father was dead too, and our only brother in South America fighting his way up in the world, and we two—it seemed strange, even after a twelvemonth, as we spoke of it— were in Rome.

And then we talked of the future : how I was to paint a great picture which should take the world by storm, and be hung on the line at the Academy by unanimous accla- mation of all the Hanging Committee the moment it was seen : and how I was to build the most artistic house that ever had been conceived, and fill it with beautiful old furniture and tapestry and china : and how my studio was to be besieged by eager buyers : and how I was never to accept a commission 'even for hundreds of pounds,' as Lucy said (her ideas of the value of

money were very rudimentary in those days;
and I believe a hundred pounds stood in her
mind as an algebraic x, or symbol of an
unknown quantity), unless I thoroughly
liked the subject and felt it to be worthy of
artistic treatment.

Generally, Lucy's part in these prophetic
visions was to marry somebody ' very nice,'
and have a charming house near mine—not
too artistic ; for Lucy had private objections
to certain dull blues, and dingy greens, and
tattered hangings which she had heard
painters incomprehensibly admire — and
several lovely children whose portraits I
was to paint. But to-night—I thought of
it after she had gone to bed—she said no
word as to her own future.

CHAPTER II.

SIGNOR SANDRO did not dissuade me from going to the Palazzo Corleoni. He smiled a little grimly when he heard of the works of art in preparation for the bazaar.

'I suppose you are to do the work, and the Principessina is to take all the praise,' said he.

'I care nothing about the praise, master; but I cannot afford to work without pay. I might be studying, doing something to improve myself, instead of daubing banalities on pasteboard screens. And if I give up my time to Donna Laura, I must have some equivalent.'

'You don't consider "the honour" to be an equivalent ?' asked Signor Sandro, looking over his maulstick at me with his gray bushy eyebrows drawn together.

'Not in the least. I think I understand pretty well what that honour is worth.'

'I think you do, Caterina !' returned my master. And he took a pinch of snuff with a long-drawn sniff of satisfaction.

'I don't much like the Corleonis,' said I. 'They impose on Lucy. They pay her very poorly, and get more work out of her than is just. She is such a soft-hearted, grateful little creature that a kind word will make her do anything.'

Signor Sandro shrugged his shoulders. 'If you make yourself a sheep, the wolf will eat you,' he answered drily. He was a good man ; but he was not quite free from the national tendency to confound soft-heartedness with thick-headedness. He was theoretically intolerant, and contemptuous of people who allowed themselves to be imposed upon. But in practice he was the gentlest of beings ; and little children tyrannized over him confidently.

We went on working in silence for a while, and then he said, ' No ; I see no reason why you should not go and earn a few francs at Palazzo Corleoni. The Princess is not a bad woman — bigoted and prejudiced, but not a bad woman. I remember her very handsome, too, thirty years ago. They tell me she has taken to devotion in these days, but still '—with a quaint apologetic inflection of voice, and with perfect seriousness—' *still* I don't think she's a bad woman.'

So I consented to go to the Palazzo Corleoni on the next Wednesday. I had been
there once or twice before, to settle Lucy's
engagement as English teacher. It is a
splendid edifice, with a noble courtyard and
staircase, all on the vast scale seen only in
Rome. But it is chill and gloomy despite
its grandeur. If one had to paint it, one
would spread crimson cloth over the marble
steps, and populate them with figures in
picturesque mediæval costume, to give some
idea of warmth and life. The withered old
porter at the entrance, in his silver-laced
livery and cocked hat, looked misanthropi-
cally out on to the street from under the
cavernous archway. All the inmates of
Palazzo Corleoni looked misanthropic when
their eyes were turned towards the street.
That was the tone of their party, the proper
thing to do. The outer world was changed

and abominable since the year 1870, and not to be contemplated without disgust. Even the great tortoiseshell cat, licking her whiskers in the midst of one small patch of sunshine in the courtyard, had a Tartuffian air of victimhood.

The Prince and Princess Bastiani-Corleoni did not occupy the whole of their huge palace, nor half, nor a quarter of it. The first floor was let to a foreign cardinal of great wealth, and the third to a rich American family, who paid highly for the privilege of putting the address of the Palazzo Corleoni on their visiting-cards. The Prince and Princess themselves inhabited a suite of rooms in the second story. This suite of rooms, however, ran along the whole front and one wing of the palace, and had as many cubic feet of space in it as would have furnished forth two or three London mansions. The

Corleonis were not very rich in proportion to their rank, but they contrived to keep up a wonderful show of outward grandeur.

Lucy and I toiled up the long marble staircase to the second story; and, in answer to her modest little ring, were admitted into a large and lofty entrance hall, with great swinging leathern doors, such as you see in Continental churches. Gloom, cold, and *ennui* seemed to inhabit that entrance-hall. The marble pavement shot out icy gleams, here and there, in the subdued light. A vast carved settee of time-blackened walnut-wood nearly filled one side of the hall, and on the other was an antique marble chimney-piece rising half-way to the vaulted roof; but the hearth beneath it was walled up, and a brazier full of wood ashes set in the middle of the floor, mocked numbed fingers and chill feet with a miserable pretence of warmth. Beyond the leather door at the further end of this vestibule there was an antechamber, carpeted and curtained, and therefore less inhuman in its aspect than the outer hall, but still bearing the impress of a formal rigidity devoid of all that goes to make up home. After that came a long suite of reception-rooms, which the beneficent sun himself had touched with some genial kindness, and whose atmosphere, therefore, a little thawed one's spirits frozen by that terrible north-west passage through the hall and antechamber. But as for 'home,' these rooms, too, proclaimed their ignorance of that blessed word, in every fold of their stiff velvet draperies, in every glittering ray from their gilded picture-frames, in every line of their satin chairs and couches disposed at right angles with each other, and their ormolu tables unacquainted with books, and adorned chiefly with the tawdry, faded *bon-bonnières* levied last New Year's Day by more or less voluntary contribution from the Princess's bachelor acquaintance. A grand pianoforte, left open in one corner of a huge, tasteless, gorgeous saloon, seemed to show its teeth at us. The whole atmosphere of the place depressed and chilled me, and I said as much to Lucy as we marched side by side through the rooms in the wake of the servant who was to announce us.

'Oh!' said she with a little look of surprise and disappointment, 'I always think this suite is so splendid. And it is never very cold here, Catherine, so that must be your fancy. The sun shines on this side of the house all day long.'

'Then it is the moral climate that does not agree with me.'

' 'Sh, dear ! Here we are at the school-room.'

We entered a room somewhat smaller than the others, but still of ample size, looking on to the courtyard. It had a few squares of common drugget disposed here and there on the brick floor, a horrible blue and yellow paper on the walls, and at one end a glazed book-case filled with school-books. On a large square table in the middle of the room stood a common office inkstand and a pounce-box, whose contents were spilt about over the green baize table-cover. There were also two or three exercise books, a dictionary, and a litter of papers. Such was the ' still life' of the picture.

Two little girls—with long growing limbs like young colts, sallow faces and soft dark eyes—sat at the table engaged with their lessons. In the embrasure of one of the windows was set an easel, and in front of the easel stood Donna Laura Corleoni, the eldest daughter of the house. She was a handsome girl, with a fine rich tint in her cheeks like the tone of a damask rose, glossy dark hair, white teeth, and a pair of rather small, but very vivacious, black eyes. Her figure was singularly upright, and the carriage of her head in particular so erect, as to give her the air of perpetually looking over an invisible stiff cravat at one, which injured the grace of her appearance in my eyes.

She came forward and greeted us, speaking English with considerable fluency and perfect self-confidence. Her manner was not unpleasant, except for an odd strain in it which I find it difficult to describe, but which I felt distinctly: she spoke to me and looked at me with an undisguised frank air of examination, as who should say, 'Now let me see what *you* are like !' but with no more apparent conception that she herself was exposed to an answering examination, than one might feel in contemplating some strange animal.

'These are my drawings, you see,' she said. 'But there is not time for me to finish all before the bazaar. I have still three screens and a box in *carton* which need to be painted, and these we must have by the end of the month. It is so important that mamma's stall be well filled, you know.'

I could not perceive that it was of any importance to me whether the Princess's stall were full or empty ; so I merely bowed my head and said nothing. Donna Laura looked at me with her quick black eyes as if she expected me to speak ; but, finding that I remained silent, she went on : 'Well, you see what is to do, Meess Wilson. And for my own sketches, if you have some advice to give——'

This was rather an awkward question. There was ability in the young lady's work : a certain decision and sense of effect. Indeed, there was so much proof of ability, that the temptation passed through my mind to give her the sincerest advice I could, which would have been to throw all these things on the fire, lock up her colour-box for six months, and begin to study drawing seriously. But of course such an utterance on my part was out of the question. I limited myself to that portion of the matter which immediately concerned me, and answered, 'I do not know whether you will think it worth while to employ me to paint these screens, Donna Laura. My time is of some value, and perhaps, as it is for a charity, you might prefer to get some friend

to assist you who has leisure to do this sort
of thing gratis.'

Lucy coloured and looked nervous at this
plain speaking; but Donna Laura displayed
no such sensitiveness.

She replied : ' Oh, we would like that they
should be very well done ; because mamma's
stall will be one of the best.   You will talk
with mamma by-and-by about the price.
Now tell me, would you line this with red
silk or blue silk ?'

I drew nearer to the light, and was bend-
ing down my head to consider the point
when I heard the door open and someone
come into the room.   Thinking it might be
the Princess, I turned round to look, and
saw Don Vittorio Corleoni.

I knew him well enough by sight.   He
was to be seen on the Pincian every afternoon at the fashionable hour in the fashion-

able season ; and once or twice in the spring
when I was making a study near the tomb
of Cecilia Metella, I had seen him pass by
on horseback. He rode well, and I had remarked him and his horse as a handsome
pair of animals. He did not look quite so
well off his horse as on it, for his legs—
pitilessly displayed by the tight - fitting,
fashionable trousers that he wore—appeared
weak and 'weedy,' like the limbs of a rickety
child. But his face was undoubtedly very
handsome. He had sharply-cut features, a
clear pale skin, hair and whiskers arranged
after the English fashion, and of that rich
blonde hue which one sees in Venetian
pictures, and a pair of eyes like sapphires.
A very handsome face, in truth, but one
which I disliked and mistrusted with an
irresistible repulsion. The leading charac-
teristic which stamped it was, I should say,

a cruel, thin-lipped sort of sensuality. The forehead was rather weak, but not dull. What those sapphire-blue eyes did see, they saw clearly, microscopically—accurately perceptive of the animalculæ in a glass of water, hopelessly blind to the stars. Let no one appeal to that face for sympathy with the higher sentiments!—it did not believe in their existence. But, still, inasmuch as a sane human creature can scarcely exist without some grain of imagination, I discovered later that even Don Vittorio Corleoni possessed a small modicum of that faculty, and he expended it all on one object: the greatness and prosperity of the princely House of Bastiani-Corleoni. That was his ideal in life. Everything else that he recognised could be touched or tasted.

Donna Laura asked her brother what he wanted, with her brisk, martinet air, which contrasted oddly with his feline quietude of manner and soft drawling voice. What did he want? He wanted a letter deciphered and translated: another from the horse-dealer in Yorkshire. Could Laura do it? If not, perhaps Meess Lucy would be kind enough?

'Meess Lucy' held out her hand for the letter with alacrity. 'Oh, I shall be very glad. It is no trouble at all,' she murmured shyly. There was a tremulous smile on her lips, and a light in her innocent eyes, which gave me a dull pain at the heart.

'This is Meess Lucy's sister, Meess Wilson,' said Donna Laura, speaking in Italian, and indicating me to her brother with a wave of the hand.

Don Vittorio drew his heels close together, and made me a grave formal bow. I was conscious that my salutation in return was

stiff and awkward. I was altogether ill at
ease. After one cool glance of inspection
Don Vittorio withdrew his attention from
me altogether; that is to say, he withdrew
his eyes from me. But I felt that he
observed me furtively. From that moment
whenever we two met, we watched one
another mistrustfully.

'You must not interrupt us, Vittorio,'
said Donna Laura. 'We are very busy,
Meess Wilson and I. And you know how
important it is that mamma's stall should
be splendid. I cannot attend to you now.
Meess Wilson and I are going to mamma to
speak of business. Come, Meess Wilson.
Make haste with your letter, Vittorio. You
know you waste the children's English hour
with all this tiresome affair of your horse.
And mamma would not be pleased if she
knew it.'

Donna Laura walked off, motioning me to follow her. I had no choice but to do so. 'I shall come back here before I go away, Lucy,' I said quickly. Lucy did not hear me. She had her head bent down over Don Vittorio's letter, whilst that patrician gentleman stood very near the school-table, stroking his youngest sister's hair, and gazing admiringly at Lucy's delicate little hand as it lay on the green cloth under his eyes.

CHAPTER III.

MAÎTRESSE FEMME.

THE Princess drove a hard bargain. I think
we should not have come to terms at all,
but for my desire to frequent that unin-
viting schoolroom in the Palazzo Corleoni
and see for myself how things went there.
But when the Princess said it was one of
the conditions of the arrangement that I
should come and work in her house, and not
carry away any of the objects which were
to be painted, the temptation was too strong
for me, and I accepted very miserable pay
rather than give the thing up. I could

think of no better course of conduct to
pursue than quietly and carefully to watch
over Lucy, and endeavour to judge of her
feeling towards Don Vittorio, without yielding to any rash impulse of anger or suspicion.

For suspicion, in truth, I had no tangible
grounds ; nothing that I could have told to
a third person without the risk of my words
either being disregarded, or having an ex-
aggerated importance attached to them.
And this latter was a result which I should
most earnestly endeavour to avoid. The
only person in whom I could confide any
trouble or perplexity which assailed me—
the only friend, indeed, I had in Rome—was
my master, Alessandro Santi ; and I would
have trusted his judgment on most subjects
as fully as I trusted the goodness of his intentions towards my sister and myself. But

on this subject—no ; I knew enough of
Italian modes of thought to be sure that
Signor Sandro would put but one inter-
pretation on Don Vittorio's visits to the
schoolroom. But this was not all. Signor
Sandro would infallibly assume that those
visits implied to Lucy's mind all, or nearly
all, that they implied to his own. My
shrewd old master much approved of the
superior freedom granted to English girls as
compared with the restraints placed upon
Italian girls, although his notions about it
were very imperfect ; but he drew several
erroneous inferences from that which he did
know. One of these inferences was that an
English girl, accustomed to mingle freely in
society instead of being shut up in a convent,
and brought out thence to be married, must
necessarily have a copious knowledge of the
world—a phrase which I have generally

found to be a euphemism for 'knowledge of
the evil things in the world.' The mixture
of simplicity, fearlessness, and romance in a
character like Lucy's was beyond his com-
prehension. He could have conceived a
nun - taught Roman schoolgirl falling an
innocent victim to Don Vittorio's fascina-
tions, but not a bright, capable, English girl
who trotted about the streets of Rome un-
attended, and read the newspapers ; whereas
the convent-bred imagination would in all
probability have taken the alarm first. To
it men in general were wolves, and young
girls only to be saved from them by im-
plicit obedience to their experienced pastors,
spiritual and temporal. How could a mind
so taught weave a web of romantic fancies
about such a one as Don Vittorio Alfonso
de' Principi Corleoni ?—a gossamer, fairy-
like, moonlit tissue of girlish dreams and

vague tenderness, no more like conscious passion than the cool glitter of Hesperus is like the fires of Etna!

Yet some such dream it was that I feared for Lucy. Or rather I feared the awakening from it that must come. The worship of 'some bright particular star' is often a not unsweet prelude in a young girl's heart to the deeper music of real love. But suddenly to find that your star is but a coarse flame fed by foul tallow—to feel the wings of your spirit scorched and withered in its glare and stench—that is a hideous experience which I was resolved to spare my Lucy at almost any cost and by almost any effort.

But then, after all, it might be that I was mistaken and over-anxious. I kept this alternative before my mind as a possibility, and for awhile all my observations seemed to tend towards raising it to a probability.

I went daily to the Palazzo Corleoni to work for Donna Laura, and to help her in her work. I found that we were not to paint in the schoolroom, but in a small cabinet near to the Princess's boudoir, so that she could easily come in and inspect our progress, which she did very often. But although I was thus not constantly with Lucy, I was within reach of her, and frequently had an opportunity of going into the schoolroom ; for the two younger girls had undertaken, as their contribution to the bazaar, to colour and gild some initial letters on cardboard, copied from an old illuminated missal, and this performance I was asked to superintend. This had not been in the bond when the Princess engaged me, but I was only too willing to make frequent visits to the schoolroom where the little girls were at work, so long as Lucy was there also. My presence there was never unwelcome, because, as Donna Laura candidly observed, the children improved in talking English at the same time that they worked at their illuminations, both Lucy and I being strictly enjoined never to converse with them but in our own language.

During all this time I never once found Don Vittorio in the schoolroom. But I saw him occasionally, nevertheless. He would lounge in of a morning to look at our drawings, and to criticise his sister's with fraternal severity. About mine he said nothing, and appeared scarcely to see them. Only once, in an access, as it seemed, of ill-temper, he remarked to Donna Laura that she was a fool to allow her performances to be exhibited in juxtaposition with mine. Donna

Laura answered very good-humouredly that she had no pretensions to be an artist like Meess Wilson, who was a favourite pupil of Professor Santi.

The Princess chanced to overhear these two speeches as she was coming into the painting-room. She chanced to overhear a great many of the speeches made in her house, and I was often struck by the familiar knowledge she displayed of things said and done out of her presence. On this occasion she gave Don Vittorio a little lecture, saying that Laura had no need to be ashamed of her work, no matter how poor it might be from an artistic point of view, for that her pious motive in doing it rendered it worth something in the eyes of all good persons ; and that, moreover, since the Holy Father himself expressly approved the object of the bazaar, she thought it would be becoming in everybody to avoid all spirit of levity in thinking or speaking of it.

The Princess's manner was very smooth, but I thought I detected a steely hardness underneath the velvet. The expression of her haughty features and dark stern eyes was not in harmony with the pious humility of her words. In short, she seemed to me to be like an able actress determined on playing a part for which nature had not fitted her. In observing her Signor Sandro's words recurred to me: 'They tell me she has *taken to devotion* in these days.' Her devotion, however, did not interfere with her mundane affairs. She governed her household with a strict rule and the most minute knowledge of details. I do not believe that her cook or her steward could have succeeded in cheating her out of a farthing. If they did peculate, after the manner of their kind, she knew it, and knew the precise extent of their peculations. But if it suited her to appear blind to them, she would shut her eyes at the proper moment without the smallest scruple, and with as little compunction would she accuse and expose the culprit the moment his misdeeds went beyond the limit she had mentally assigned to them as tolerable. I think she carried out this method in dealing with her children. For example, Don Vittorio (who was her favourite) had a great deal of apparent freedom and independence ; but I was persuaded from the first that the Princess kept a certain power in her own hands, and that however long her son's tether might be, still he was tethered. As to the Prince Bastiani-Corleoni, he was, for me, as invisible a potentate as the Mikado of Japan. I heard from others that he was a mild-mannered gentleman of handsome presence and orthodox principles, whose chief occupation in life was to audit and pass the accounts prepared for him by his wife in her vigilant management of their estate, and whose chief pastime was shooting over the domain he possessed in a distant part of the Maremma, where the wild birds throve and the peasants languished in the malaria.

After the little reproof to Don Vittorio which I have mentioned, the Princess turned to me and said, ' Ah, you are a pupil of Sandro Santi ?' (She had known this fact perfectly, long ago.) ' He is a very clever painter, and, I am told, even a better master.'

' He is a rabid " Red,"' observed Don Vittorio in a tone of cold contempt. ' When we had a government he was banished as dangerous. I suppose now he is considered a shining light—or, at least, no worse than the rest.'

I took no more heed of this speech than if I had been stone deaf, but went on painting steadily, conscious all the time that the Princess was watching me as steadily. She made a pause before speaking, as though she thought it possible that I might take up the glove thus openly thrown down by her son ; but when she finally spoke she did so in the tone of one answering on an instant impulse :

'Oh, my son !' she said, 'do not let us forget Christian charity in our judgment even of those who are misguided enough to rebel against their sovereign and father. What you speak of happened long ago. Perhaps years have brought better counsel to Santi. He is getting old now, and very

likely repents the errors of his youth. Let
us hope so.'

I had an instinctive feeling that she
expected this speech to call forth some reply
from me. But I took no more heed of it
than of Don Vittorio's, painting on steadily,
with the Princess watching me steadily, as
before.

For the first week she did not talk much
to me during her visits to the painting-
room. I think she was observing me, and
trying to read my character. After a while
she began to converse with me, always
putting direct questions, and not betraying
any annoyance (although I think she felt
some) at the laconic brevity of my answers.
In this fashion, and by a methodically
regular process, she catechized me about
my history, and learned the little there was
to know—as, for instance, that I had studied

drawing in England before my father's death; that my father had been an architect ; that I had a small yearly income between me and destitution ; that Lucy inherited a sum of two thousand pounds from her mother ; that I hoped to follow the profession of a painter, and had come to Rome with the view of qualifying myself to do so ; and that I had had an introduction to Santi from my old Italian teacher, who knew him years ago. I was amused to find afterwards that she had previously cross-questioned Lucy in precisely the same manner, and had evidently examined me with the intention of comparing and sifting our statements.

The effect produced on Lucy by this sort of catechism was very different from that which it made on me. She accepted the Princess's questioning as a proof of kindly interest in us. And it was true that that

haughty dame treated Lucy with much
more sweetness of manner than she thought
it worth while to bestow on me. She had
managed to soothe Lucy's natural timidity
and to conquer her shyness, and that once
done, it was not difficult to win some affection
from her. There never was a nature which
responded more immediately to the least
show of kindness than my sister's. And
the facility with which she fell under the
influence of those around her was a weakness in her character which I was sure the
Princess Corleoni had not failed to perceive.
And then the query presented itself to my
mind, What motive could the Princess have
for influencing and attracting Lucy?

I puzzled over this riddle, turning and
twisting it this way and that, and never
coming to a satisfactory solution. A year
or two ago I should simply have accepted

the Princess's kind, caressing manner to my
sister as the most natural thing in the world,
which needed no explanation. Lucy was
used to being petted and spoken softly to
from a little child. But my year's residence
in Rome had made me suspicious of such
behaviour on the part of such a woman
as the haughty Princess Olympia. Sometimes, however, I went back to my old
simple way of looking at things. Why
should not the Princess be kind to Lucy
solely because she liked the girl's soft ways
and sweet looks? Then again I rejected
this idea, and told myself that a thousand
minute circumstances tended to show that
the Princess was carrying out a line of
conduct dictated by calculation rather than
feeling. Once or twice the wild notion
darted into my mind that the Princess
perceived Don Vittorio's admiration for

Lucy, and was inclined to yield to her son's wishes in the matter ; she harped a good deal on Lucy's little fortune, and one day used the phrase, ' a nice *dot*,' or dowry, in speaking of it. But of course such a notion *was* wild, and not to be entertained in sober seriousness. Poor Lucy's money could not possibly offer any temptations to such people as the Corleonis ; the interest of it would not pay Don Vittorio's tailor for half a year. Besides, she was a girl of no family, giving lessons for pay, a foreigner, and—worse than all—a heretic ! No—no ; the thing was too outrageously absurd and improbable, and could only have flitted into a brain weary and perplexed with unavailing ponderings on one subject.

Before the day of the great bazaar arrived, however, I had got hold of a clue to the enigma.

CHAPTER IV.

WHEN I look back on that period of my
employment in the Palazzo Corleoni, it
seems to have extended over a long time ;
and yet the dates in a little diary, or
memorandum-book, which I kept then show
that barely three weeks elapsed from the
first day to the last of my engagement.
But the time seemed long to me then, and
seems long in the retrospect, because several
incidents of great interest in my life were
crowded into it.

I did not neglect the object which had

chiefly induced me at first to go to the
Palazzo Corleoni—namely, to see for myself
what terms Don Vittorio was on with my
sister, whether he visited the schoolroom
daily, and to watch his behaviour towards
Lucy with jealous scrutiny. But it was not
possible, of course, that I should devote
myself wholly to that object. Having
undertaken to make certain drawings, I was
bound to execute them to the best of my
ability, and honestly to fulfil my part of the
bargain by helping and counselling Donna
Laura. And besides, as I have said, I was
not free to be in my sister's company whensoever it pleased me to seek it. Still, I
flattered myself that my opportunities for
observation were sufficient to assure me that
Don Vittorio took no special pains to see
Lucy. And I began to think that I had
altogether over-estimated the danger to her

peace of mind from the attention bestowed
on her by those handsome, inscrutable,
sapphire-tinted eyes. I had refrained from
hinting my fears and surmises to Lucy. If
she were fancy free it was not for me to
trouble the innocent serenity of her mind.
If she were indulging in any girlish romance,
open interference and opposition might put
her into an attitude of antagonism towards
me, which would weaken my influence over
her, and diminish my means of standing
between her and sorrow.

She talked to me freely enough, when
we were at home of an evening, about the
Corleonis—about the Princess especially,
whose virtues and piety she descanted on at
length. And sometimes she would use a
phraseology in speaking of them which
instantly struck on my ear as being foreign
to Lucy's usual way of talking, and which I

was convinced she had caught and unconsciously imitated from somebody. Possibly
it was from the Princess herself, I thought,
who habitually used a certain pietistic jargon
peculiar to her Church. Every Church has
its own, I suppose. At least, I knew that
such was the case with more than one
dissenting sect in my native town, and now
I found that the orthodox and strictly
Catholic Romans had plenty of sentences
and turns of speech ready cut and dried
for use in discoursing on religious matters.
Some of these were almost as purely
technical as Signor Sandro's studio talk,
and always suggested to my mind something
unpleasantly mechanical and prosaic. Lucy,
however, did not feel them to be so. She
was less critical—perhaps less hard—than
I. Then, too, the Princess's partiality
flattered her—simple-hearted child that she

was! And certainly that partiality seemed to increase daily. Lucy was frequently invited to sit with the Princess in her boudoir whilst Donna Laura and I were painting, and she generally was bidden to remain there even during the visits of certain exalted personages who were amongst the Princess Olympia's most intimate and valued guests. Such a degree of favour was never extended to me—to my inward thankfulness! And why—*why*, I wondered more and more day by day, was it bestowed on Lucy?

One afternoon the Princess entered the painting-room, where her daughter and I were at work, and said with an impressive air, 'Laura, his Eminence would like to see some of your drawings. He is very much interested and pleased to hear that you are working so well for our bazaar. Bring them into the boudoir. Madame de Clavigny is there, too.'

Donna Laura prepared to obey, and began to divest herself of the holland blouse which she wore whilst painting. The Princess turned back to me as if struck by an after-thought, and said, ' Would you like to bring some of your drawings also, Mcess Wilson ?'

' If you will excuse me, madam, I would rather go on with my work. The daylight hours are few and precious.'

I thought the Princess looked by no means displeased at my refusal. ' As you please, as you please,' she said, with a gracious bend of the head. But Donna Laura, with a good honest impulse, insisted that I should come too, and display a pair of hand-screens of my painting, which she thought particularly well executed. ' You know,' said she, ' Madame de Clavigny is

very rich and very fond of buying pretty
things, and who knows but she may give
you an order for a picture ? You always
say you want to earn money. Don't throw
away a chance. I shall tell her that you
have done the best things and helped me
with mine.'

With all her bluntness and absence of
suavity, I had long ago discovered that
Donna Laura had some kindness of heart ;
and her character impressed me as being
incomparably more lovable than that of any
other member of the family with whom I
was acquainted.

'It is kind of you to consider my interests,
Donna Laura,' said I hesitatingly. At that
moment I caught a look of annoyance on
the Princess's face which determined my
decision. I am ashamed to own that a
sentiment of rebellion against the Princess's

velvet-gloved iron will was a stronger motive
for displaying my work in the boudoir than
any hope of selling a picture to Madame de
Clavigny. It was childish, perhaps, but I
could not help saying to myself, ' You *shan't*
have your own way this time ! I'll take
you at your word.' So I finished my
answer to Donna Laura thus : ' And, as
you say, it would be foolish to throw away
a chance. I will work an extra half hour
for you to-morrow, if I lose a little daylight
now.'

I think that if Donna Laura had been
looking at her lady mother's face at that
moment she would have repented her rash
insistance, for a cloud on that dark brow
was a formidable sight to all who lived under
the rule of Olympia Corleoni. But the girl
was happily unconscious of the cloud on this
occasion, and in an instant it had passed

away, and the Princess looked her usual composed and slightly sanctimonious self.

In the boudoir—an eye-afflicting apartment hung with damask of the colour of the yolk of an egg, on which about a dozen vilely-executed copies of well-known pictures by old masters glared from out massive gilt frames—the distinguished company was seated after the fashion of distinguished companies in thoroughly Italian houses— that is to say, the chairs were all ranged in a formal semi-circle, as if someone were presently expected to 'address the meeting.' The company on this occasion was very distinguished—all but one member of it. The undistinguished member was my little Lucy. I caught sight of her curly head directly I went in, just visible behind and above the black velvet and sables which covered the portly person of Madame de

Clavigny. This lady was the wife of a diplomat accredited to the Vatican, and was a leading personage in the orthodox and aristocratic circles of Roman society. Next to her, enthroned in the most comfortable armchair in the room, sat a tall, thin, hatchet-faced old gentleman in black ecclesiastical garb. His lean old hands, partly encased in knitted woollen mittens, were crossed on his knee, and his lean old legs in scarlet stockings were crossed one over the other, and his watery blue eyes looked very mild and not a little stupid. And this was his Eminence the Cardinal Zampini, Archbishop of Borgofosco, and a reverend pillar of the Church. Near to him, just the least trifle behind him, and within easy reach of his Eminence's ear, sat one who looked neither mild nor stupid—a certain Monsignor Chiappaforti, well known in more than one social sphere of the Eternal City. Monsignore was at present in attendance on the Cardinal—told off, as it were, to be aide-de-camp to that aged major-general of the Church Militant during the latter's stay in Rome ; for his Eminence did not reside in the capital, but had temporarily deprived his flock at Borgofosco of the light of his countenance, having some business to transact at the Vatican. Chiappaforti's round, smooth-shaven, good-humoured face was very attractive at first sight to many persons. The quality I have most frequently heard attributed to him was *bonhomie.* ' Monsignor Chiappaforti's manners have such a delightful *bonhomie* about them !' And he was undoubtedly quick-witted and well-educated. He laughed a great deal—a low, musical, seemingly spontaneous laugh. I say ' seemingly spontaneous,' because I am persuaded that he was a great deal too clever and sarcastic to be really ingenuously amused and delighted by half the things he laughed at with that air of almost infantine heartiness.

The conversation was being carried on in French in honour of Madame de Clavigny, who could speak nothing else. His Eminence did not shine particularly in the linguistic line, albeit we were told that he had passed many years in Belgium. But Monsignore spoke French very fluently, and English, and, I was told, German also, and he helped out the old Cardinal whenever he boggled for a word. In fact, he helped out every-one who showed any tendency to boggle, and altogether drove his heterogeneous team into whatsoever conversational highways or by-ways it pleased him to follow, with the ease and skill of an accomplished whip. It

must have been a hard-mouthed brute, indeed, that he could not manage, or at least
one very resolutely and earnestly bent on
going in a direction opposite to that in
which Monsignore would fain guide him.

On the present occasion everyone was
willing to talk about the same topic—the
forthcoming bazaar, namely. I, as a mere
supernumerary figure in the scene, was able
to observe it all at my ease. Donna Laura,
after having kissed his Eminence's hand—
an action which, from a girl of her age to a
white-haired pastor of her Church, seemed
to me graceful and pretty—proceeded to
display her screens and fans and cardboard
boxes before his reverend countenance whilst
he sat still in his chair. Poor old gentleman! He did his best to seem pleased, but
a more lack-lustre eye than that with which
he contemplated the various objects held up

before him one after the other it never was
my lot to see. 'Very pretty, very pretty.
Ah ! you are very clever ; yes, yes. Very
clever, indeed !' These phrases he repeated
over and over again in his mild, quavering
old voice. And, on the whole, I don't
know that he could have said anything
better. But Monsignore was a different sort
of critic. His *bravas* were also profuse, but
not so absolutely indiscriminating as those
of his Eminence, and he interspersed them
with neat little appreciative remarks on the
various subjects portrayed, which somehow
half persuaded even me that he took a lively
interest in the whole affair.

After a while it came to the turn of my
drawings to be exhibited. True to her word,
Donna Laura specially called Madame de
Clavigny's attention to them, and un-
grudgingly gave me full credit for all I

had done to help her. My pictures had
also the honour to be submitted to the gaze
of the Cardinal. I was sorry for him, so
evidently was he bored and bewildered by
this second tax on his complaisance and
patience. But here again Monsignore came
nobly to the rescue. He was pleased to
praise my drawings in the most flattering
terms. And after one very flowery eulogium
he surprised me greatly by saying, 'I am
all the more delighted that this good work
should have been done by the sister of our
dear Signorina Lucia.' And at the same
time Lucy gave him a look of the most
beaming gratitude. Nothing delighted her
more than to hear me praised. It was a
sure way to her favour. Her pleased look,
therefore, was not surprising, but it was to
me both surprising and puzzling to find her
accepting the epithet of ' our dear Signorina

Lucia' from Monsignor Chiappaforti as a natural and accustomed form of speech. So absorbed was she in gazing on Monsignore with her trusting, innocent, grateful blue eyes that she did not observe my astonishment. Monsignore, however, observed it, and he at once repeated the words 'our dear Signorina Lucia,' looking amiably across at me. Then he bent a little closer to the Cardinal's ear and whispered a few sentences into it, of which sentences the sibilant words 'Sandro Santi' were all that I caught. Monsignore's eyes were inscrutably cast down whilst he whispered, but his Eminence instantly honoured me with an attentive, and not particularly benevolent, stare.

When Lucy and I were at home that evening, I said to her that I had been surprised to hear Monsignor Chiappaforti speak of her and to her in so familiar and

affectionate a strain, to which she answered
that he was the most kind and amiable of
beings, and treated her rather as if she were
a daughter of the house of Corleoni than as
a poor teacher who worked there for pay,
and that in all his ways and words he
presented an edifying and touching example
of Christian charity.　And the Cardinal—
was he not a dear, venerable old man?
Would I not admit that he was?　I replied
that, as to the Cardinal, I did not know
enough of him to say whether he were
'dear' or 'venerable,' but that for the
moment I was not concerned to discuss
that Prince of the Church.　Lucy, however,
still harped on his Eminence's venerable looks.

　'And I noticed,' said she, 'that you
curtsied to him very reverently when you
left the room, Catherine.　I was so glad to
see it!'

'To have done otherwise would have
been gross ill-manners, Lucy mine ; but I
assure you that my curtsy was not intended
as a tribute to Cardinal Zampini's moral
worth, about which I know absolutely
nothing. I should have treated a Mandarin
with just the same respect if I had been
presented to him in a Pekin drawing-room
by a Princess of the Celestial Empire !'

' Oh, Catherine !'

' Oh, Lucy !'

' I wish you wouldn't talk so, Catty
dear.'

' How is it that you have scarcely ever
mentioned Monsignor Chiappaforti's name
to me, and yet have become quite a dear
friend of his, as it seems ?'

' I fancied—it seemed to me as if you—
you disliked all the Princess's friends whenever I did mention them. And I think—

I do think you are prejudiced against the
Catholic clergy, Catherine. Perhaps Signor
Santi puts it into your head. He *is* a
Republican, I know ; and I am afraid he
has no religion.'

This speech made me very grave. It
was something new that Lucy should pur-
posely avoid any topic with me. We differed
by temperament, and the very constitution
of our minds, on a hundred subjects ; but
we had hitherto discussed together whatever
came into our heads with the freest confidence. For some time past I had felt the
presence of a kind of veil between my young
sister's mind and my own, although she was
as gentle and affectionate towards me as
ever. And a few days later I had another
proof of it. I chanced to see in Lucy's
bedroom—we occupied two tiny sleeping
chambers, little more than closets, one on

each side of the sitting-room—a large photograph of one of the well-known Madonnas of Giovanni Bellini. It was placed upright on the chest of drawers and caught my eye at once.

'That is a charming picture,' said I. ' Where did you get it, Lucy ?'

' The Princess gave it to me.'

' The Princess Corleoni ? You *must* be in favour ! I never heard of her giving anything to anybody. Why didn't you show it to me ?'

Lucy coloured and hesitated, but she answered at length plainly enough that she was afraid I might say something sarcastic, or might turn her picture into ridicule.

'*I* turn Giovanni Bellini into ridicule——!'

' No ; not Giovanni Bellini, Catherine, but the Madonna.'

All at once a light flashed in on me at

those words, which made everything clear in a moment. They were trying to convert her! But why—*why?*

Signor Sandro found an instant solution to this question when I hinted to him my suspicion (it was, indeed, far more than a suspicion), and told him how unhappy it made me.

'Ah, *già!*' he said very quietly, 'Lucia has fifty thousand lire of her own. A very nice little dowry to enter a religious house with.'

I lay awake for hours that night with an aching heart.

CHAPTER V.

SIGNOR SANDRO's advice was to watch and wait ; to lay secret trains for the discovery and exposure of the plot against Lucy's little patrimony (he refused to consider the matter in any other light), and then to spring a mine and blow up the plotters with a theatrical and virtue-protected-and-villainy-discovered kind of *dénouement.* He grew brisk and eager, was full of schemes, talked of renewing half-forgotten relations with this person and that person who might prove useful, and, in a word, the old conspirator in him was thoroughly re-awakened. He had passed the prime of his early manhood in conspiracy—always from patriotic motives, which approved themselves to *his* conscience, at least—and had grown to think conspiracy the proper method of fighting evil things, whether in high places or low places. He could not understand my point of view when I told him that what chiefly pained me was to find that Lucy had begun to withdraw her full confidence from me. As to her becoming a Catholic, that alone did not seem to me so great a misfortune.

'Pshaw, Caterina,' said Signor Sandro, ' you don't know what you are talking about. They'll never rest till they get her money ; and the only way to secure it, is to make her enter this pet sisterhood of theirs. Don't you know what their grand bazaar is really for ? To get funds to buy a house and grounds for their nuns. It's illegal, you say? Oh, there are ways of evading the law, never fear. They have plenty of clever heads among them.'

'It may be, master, that poor Lucy's little fortune has nothing to do with the zeal of the Princess and her friends. I have no right to say that they are conscienceless in the matter. They may be sincerely anxious to secure Lucy's eternal welfare.'

'Why are they not anxious to secure *your* eternal welfare? A soul is a soul, eh? And yet they have not made the slightest effort at converting you!'

This was an argument which certainly had some weight. For to answer that I was not so sweet and interesting a person as Lucy would scarcely have been a good reason for the indifference of devout persons as to my conversion from error!

I was silent, and Signor Sandro went on triumphantly, 'Ay, ay; you get somebody to leave you fifty thousand lire, and you'll find Monsignor Chiappaforti's interest in the state of your soul will spring up like a mushroom.' Then he proceeded to enter into a variety of stratagems for unmasking the real purposes of Monsignor Chiappaforti, and exhibiting him before Lucy's eyes in his true colours. Signor Sandro especially hated Monsignore, and considered him to be the originator of the scheme for Lucy's conversion. The Princess he spoke of far less harshly. She was not a bad woman : a bigot, of course, and under the influence of the priests ; but not a hard-hearted woman. I wondered, as I listened to him, whether any remembrance of the Princess Olympia's youthful beauty, thirty years ago, availed to soften my old master's judgment of her. If it were so, I am sure he did not know it. But I had my suspicions that the Princess's splendid eyes, and rich black tresses, and Juno-like figure—' the true Roman type!' Signor Sandro would exclaim enthusiastically, ' the true Roman type!'—were somehow accounted to her for righteousness.

After my first talk with my old friend on the subject, I lay awake for hours, as I have said, revolving painful thoughts. But the night brought counsel, and when I went to the studio early next morning I was resolved how to act. I would speak out plainly and straightforwardly to Lucy, and to the Princess, and to Monsignore himself, if I had the chance. Plots and counterplots should be thrown to the winds; and if there was to be war, I, at least, would not carry it on in ambuscade.

My firmness was put to the test instantly,

for Signor Sandro scouted the idea of this course of action, and opposed it vehemently. 'You are a fool, Caterina!' said he, shaking his brush at me indignantly ; 'a blundering fool!'

'Thanks, master.'

'Thanks, master,' he exclaimed, trying to mimic my quiet tone in one of lively irritation. 'I say that if you go on as you say, you'll lose your sister altogether. You don't know these people—I do.'

'But I know my sister.'

'Ta, ta, ta! A little white mouse! What do you think she can do against such a wily old fox as Giacomo Chiappaforti? I tell you, you must match cunning with cunning.'

'I can't do it, master.'

'You? No. You're as blunt as a barbarian! But let me do it for you.'

'No, master, I must do what I think right.'

'You think? Isn't it enough to raise the bile of a stone to hear her talk?' cried Signor Sandro. And he gradually worked himself up into such a violent passion that he fairly danced about the studio, inveighing against my obstinacy and stupidity, and knocking over the mannikin on which I had carefully arranged some crimson drapery the day before. I let him work off his fiery temper a little in these performances, and then I said: 'Listen, master: I know you are full of kind interest in me and Lucy. I am not ungrateful——'

'Oh, no! Ungrateful? What an idea! Only you are as obstinate as a mule, and intend to take your own way—gratefully.'

'Please to hear me—I have heard you. I don't believe in lies; be the intention

what it may, good or bad, wise or foolish,
I have no faith in the power of lies to help
anyone. Your own proverb says, " A lie
hath short legs." '

Signor Sandro sat down at his easel with
his back to me and pretended to be absorbed
in painting a bit of background. I went on,
nothing daunted :

'Now, if I pretend not to see what is
going on with Lucy and these people at the
Palazzo Corleoni, I shall be lying to all
intents and purposes. I have lied in that
way already by holding my tongue about——'

I paused, and I saw Signor Sandro's head
turn a very little in a listening attitude.
'Well,' said I, 'I cannot explain to you what
the matter was, but I had a suspicion, and
I smothered it up, and waited and watched,
on your plan, and no good has come of it.
I dare say a frank word would have set it

all right. Any way, I have thought about
the matter to the best of my ability, and
I have made up my mind to be absolutely
sincere. We despise wiles and tricks and
crooked ways—don't let us follow them! I
never heard of but one way to shame the
devil, and that is to tell the truth.'

The background on which Signor Sandro
was at work was assuming a very extra-
ordinary appearance. I knew that his
attention was wholly given to my words,
although he still feigned to be painting in a
rapt absorption. I went close up to him
and laid my hand on his shoulder. 'Come,
master,' said I, 'forgive my plain speaking.
I'm a blunt barbarian, as you say, but don't
hate me for that.'

For an instant he remained still, stiff, and
mute. Then all of a sudden he put up one
hand to touch mine, which lay on his shoulder,

and took a noisy pinch of snuff with the other. 'Hate you, Caterina?' he said, with a little break in his voice. 'No. You *are* a fool—remember I said so—but I don't hate you for it. I don't know—I don't know but I almost like you the better for it; but that's because I'm a fool, too.'

Dear, kind, noble-hearted, irascible old master! All the prejudices of early education, and the unfortunate influences of a youth embittered by secret struggles against injustice, could not stifle the natural loyalty and affection of his character.

That afternoon I spoke to Lucy plainly. I told her that I fancied she was inclined to be attracted by the Roman Catholic religion, and that on that subject I should not then argue with her; but that it hurt me to think she should conceal her mind from me. And I begged her to return to her old

frank confidence, promising, on my side, to
be equally unreserved with her. She looked
greatly startled at first—almost scared.
And then, with a gush of tears, she threw
her arms round my neck, exclaiming, ' Oh,
Catherine, I am so glad to be able to speak
to you. I wanted to tell you long ago.'

' And why,' said I quickly, ' did you not ?'

She was silent, hiding her tear-stained
face on my shoulder. In vain I repeated
my question, coaxing and begging her to
reply. Then I spoke more severely, asking
if that were a specimen of the confidence
she had seemed so glad to give me. Upon
this she raised her head, and there was a
look of perplexity and distress on her
innocent young face which pained me
greatly.

' Catherine,' she said, ' a promise is sacred.
Do not press me with questions I cannot

answer. I am bound by a promise. You would not wish me to break my word ?'

'No,' said I. (But I am almost afraid that I did wish it.) 'Only, my dear Lucy, make no more such promises, I implore you !'

We talked a long while after that. Lucy seemed, in truth, overjoyed to be able to speak of her religious feelings to me. They were pure feelings : innocent, devout, and loving. There was not a trace of guile, or affected piety or exaggeration about anything she said. Despite my old master's hatred and mistrust of Monsignor Chiappaforti, Signor Sandro himself would have been obliged to confess that the reverend prelate's teaching had not, at least as yet, tainted the ingenuousness of my Lucy's nature. And throughout all she said there was not a hint at any such purpose of securing her little dowry for the sisterhood as Signor Sandro suspected. Just before we parted for the night I took her pretty head between my hands, and, stroking down the wavy, bright brown locks, I said :

' But, little Lucy, they must not make a nun of you, and cut off all this curly wig I am so fond of.'

She laughed like a child.

' Make a nun of *me*, Catherine ! Oh, my dear, you little know how far short I fall of the standard of goodness needed for that holy life. Besides, I don't think such an idea has entered anyone's head.'

I at once and unreservedly believed that it had not entered *her* head, at all events. My heart was greatly lightened when I lay down in my bed that night, and I was more than ever resolved to carry out that best of all policies—honesty—in all my future dealings. I did not desire, truly, that Lucy should become a Roman Catholic. But that idea did not inspire me with any pious horror. What had seemed terrible to me was the thought that Lucy would be weaned from her old confiding love for me. I was her only friend and guardian. Our brother was in . another hemisphere, and we two were alone in a foreign country, and all our strength and comfort and safeguard lay in our mutual trust and affection. To have that undermined would be almost as great a misfortune for us both as I could well imagine. But it had not been undermined, and it should not be. My mind was more serene and untroubled than it had been since the first day of my entering the Palazzo Corleoni.

CHAPTER VI.

A TUG-OF-WAR.

In the course of the past year Lucy and I had paid a short visit to Tivoli, and had been so enchanted with the place that we both greatly desired to spend a longer time there and explore the surrounding country. We had made a plan—after due examination of our budget and discussion of ways and means—to go to Tivoli again early in the spring and stay there at least three weeks. I was to make the jaunt pay for itself in some measure, by working at a picture which had been haunting my fancy for some

time ; and Lucy had looked forward with
eagerness to the holiday and change of
scene.

For some weeks past neither of us had
mentioned the subject, but now I had a
strong additional motive, besides the expected pleasure of our trip, for wishing to
go away from Rome for a time, and to make
a break in that habit of almost daily inter-
course with the Corleonis which I knew
had strongly helped to bring Lucy's flexible
nature under the Princess's influence. I
proposed to my sister to make our trip to
Tivoli immediately after the completion of
my work for Donna Laura. I should have
finished what I had undertaken to do by
the end of that same week. Why should
we not set off at once ?

'So soon, Catherine?' said Lucy doubtfully.

'Why not? Next Saturday will be the last day but one of March. It is a lovely time for the country.'

'Will it not be cold there?'

'I think not. You know we were there last year quite at the beginning of April, and the weather was delightful.'

'It seems rather sudden. Why are you in such haste to go, Catherine?'

'I might answer that I want to get to work on my picture, that the aspect of the landscape at this season is precisely what I require for my background, and that I feel the change of scene would be good for my health. All these answers would be true in themselves, but yet they would not give you my strongest motive for wishing to go away at once. I shall tell you the whole truth, Lucy: I especially desire to take you for a time out of reach of the Princess and Mon-

signor Chiappaforti and their circle. If
their teachings are worth anything, they
will stand the test of a fortnight's peaceful
and unbiased meditation. It shall be unbiased, so far as I am concerned, for I give
you my word not to enter into the discussion
of any religious subjects whatever whilst we
are away.'

Nothing more was said at that time.
The next morning we were both employed
at the Palazzo Corleoni, and in the afternoon
Lucy timidly said to me that she did not
think she should be able to go to Tivoli so
soon as I wished.

' Why not ?' I asked.

' I do not think I shall be able to get a
holiday from my lessons to Francesca and
Livia.'

' *I* will see to that.'

' The Princess is very unwilling that

their English studies should be interrupted.'

'I suppose that events sometimes happen
in spite of the Princess's unwillingness. I
wish very much—*very* much—that you
should go with me to Tivoli at the end of
March. I have honestly told you all my
reasons for wishing you to go. Whether
the Princess has with equal honesty stated
all her reasons for wishing you to stay, I
don't know. But I think you will not
refuse to please me, Lucy. I have not
often asked you to sacrifice your wishes to
mine.'

'My own dear Catherine, I would do
anything I could to please you, indeed—
indeed. I *will* go, Catty! I will go—if I
may.'

I had an uneasy suspicion that this 'if I
may' did not refer solely to the Princess's

consent that Francesca and Livia should have a fortnight's holiday from their English lessons. Had matters gone so far that Lucy was in subjection to Monsignor Chiappaforti's will as to her going or staying? I was resolved to keep the straightforward path I had marked for myself, and after a minute's reflection I told Lucy that I should take an early opportunity of speaking to Monsignore himself on the subject.

'Shall you, Catherine?' she said, looking at me with wide-open eyes and an air half of alarm, half of admiration at my boldness. But she made no attempt to dissuade me.

It was very well to talk of taking an early opportunity of speaking to Monsignore, but how was I to get at him? I was not acquainted with his haunts and his habits; and nothing would be easier than for the Princess Corleoni to prevent me from meeting

him in her house, if she were so minded.
It came into my head that Donna Laura
might help me ; and the inspiration proved
to be a good one, for she at once said that
she believed Monsignore came to the Palazzo
every afternoon about three o'clock on business connected with the bazaar, and that if I
wished to speak with him she would let him
know it, and ask him to receive me. No
sooner said than done. She walked straight
into her mother's boudoir, and returned in a
few minutes saying that Monsignore was
alone and would be happy to see me.

I found him seated at the Princess's
writing-table with a bundle of letters before
him and several packets of tickets. There
were also some printed circulars respecting
the great bazaar, setting forth its object,
and giving a list of the ladies who had consented to patronize it and hold stalls. The

reverend gentleman had apparently been correcting these forms for the printer, for the one which lay before him had several marks on the margin of it.

'Good-morning—good-morning, Signorina,' said he, with a very gracious bow and pleasant smile. 'Here I am busy at the " great work," you see. Upon my word, I shall be glad when this affair is over. You have no idea of the amount of my time it has occupied. Let us hope that we shall do some good by it after all. I am in good hopes for the result. Our ladies have been exemplary—exemplary in their zeal. And I'm sure we have to thank *you* immensely for—— Will you not take a seat?'

He was very easy, very smiling, very loquacious. He looked at me with an unconscious, genial air, as if he had not a project in the world deeper than the selling

of many tickets for the charitable Fancy
Fair, nor a suspicion that I could have anything disagreeable to say to him.

'Monsignore,' said I, 'I know you are
always busy, and I should not have intruded
on your time——'

'No intrusion, Signorina,' he interrupted,
with a bow and the most beaming of smiles.

'Well, I mean that I should not have
asked to speak with you except from a
strong and serious motive. And now you
have been so kind as to give me the opportunity of doing so, I will try to spare your
time and my own by being brief and speaking
to the point, without compliments.'

'Admirable!' he murmured, almost as if
he were speaking to himself. 'Ah, my dear
young lady, I wish more of your amiable sex
had your good sense and consideration. I
have had a long and extensive experience of

the female character—a beautiful character, full of qualities which command our tenderness and respect—but I must own that the feminine intellect, so far as my observation goes, has a tendency to be discursive. Want of concentration—eh ?' And Monsignore laughed his child-like laugh as if he were heartily amused, although, in truth, I could see nothing specially humorous in what he had said.

'Monsignore, you have acquired a great influence over my sister Lucy. You want to convert her to Roman Catholicism ; I want her not to be converted. But I am no bigot, and I do not pretend to say that I should break my heart if she were received into your Church to-morrow.'

Monsignore had leant back in his chair when I began to speak, and with his hands calmly folded on the table before him, and his eyes cast down, nodded gently at each sentence, as who should say, ' I am giving you all my attention.' I thought the last clause somewhat surprised him, however, although the expression of surprise which passed over his features—if, indeed, I had rightly read it as such — was but momentary.

' That,' said he very softly, ' is a weakness inherent in heresy, which you, my dear young lady, have the noble candour to acknowledge, but to which many Protestants are blind. Once cast yourself loose from the anchor of infallible authority, and you drift about in endless uncertainty. It must ever be with very different feelings from those which you own to, that a Catholic could behold one he loved leaving the true Church for any other.'

' Monsignore, I have taken to heart your

words about the discursiveness of the female intellect, and I mean to stick to the point.'

'*Brava!*' he murmured very blandly. But the quick glance he shot at me was scarcely so bland.

'The point is this : I wish my sister Lucy to accompany me on a short visit to Tivoli at the end of this month ; she has expressed her willingness to do so, " if she may ;" and I, surmising her consent to be contingent on yours, have come to ask whether you mean to oppose her going, and if so, why.'

' Really, my dear young lady, you surprise me ! Why should you suppose that *I* wish to oppose your sister's going to Tivoli ? Now, *why?* Pray tell me. I am quite curious to know.' And again Monsignore laughed very sweetly.

' It is scarcely worth while, Monsignore,

to waste your time in giving all the reasons which induced me——'

'Ah now, pray tell me. I assure you I am quite in the dark. And as to wasting my time, I have now some half-hour of leisure.'

'But I have not, Monsignore. I must return to Donna Laura.'

'Oh, come, come, Signorina! You must not balk my curiosity. Donna Laura is not such a tyrant. Besides, I will give you plenary absolution for robbing her of a few minutes, ha, ha, ha!'

I found there was no hope of inducing him to answer my question until I had first answered his. So, as briefly and directly as I could, I told him that I had gathered from Lucy's manner that someone who strongly influenced her opposed her going to Tivoli ; that I did not believe this person

to be the Princess, or at least I did not
believe the Princess to be acting without
superior orders in the matter ; and that I
had guessed the real opponent to be Monsignor Chiappaforti, and his object to be
that of preventing the impression he had
made on my sister's mind from being
weakened by a fortnight's absence, and by
the influence of an heretical sister to whom
she was attached.

'Upon my word, Signorina, you are more
frank than flattering ! You are making me
out a sort of Macchiavelli—as you English
understand Macchiavelli. Now I should
have thought, Miss Wilson, that your
strength of mind would have been superior
to the vulgar prejudices in vogue amongst
some of your countrymen. You have been
thinking of me as a sort of bugbear—the
type of the " Jesuit priest " whom your

Evangelical clergymen discourse about in
Exeter Hall. You surprise me—you surprise me very much.'

I believed that I had surprised him ; but
I did not believe that it was my opinion of
himself which surprised him, nor even my
bluntness in expressing it. There was
evidently something else which puzzled him.
And all the while he was talking about
Macchiavelli and Jesuits, I felt convinced
that he attached no importance to what he
was saying, but had his mind full of some
other thought.

' Well, now, Monsignore, I have answered
your question ; will you answer mine ? Do
you mean to persuade Lucy not to go to
Tivoli ?'

' Tut, tut! *I* persuade her——! Suppose,
however, I were to say " Yes." What
then ?'

'Then I should be frightened ; because I should take it as a proof that you were resolved to separate Lucy from me to the utmost of your power.'

'You frightened ! The strong-minded Miss Wilson frightened ! You are pleased to laugh at me, my dear young lady.'

'I am far enough from laughing, Monsignore. I should be frightened. And if I were thoroughly frightened, I should run away.'

I had certainly surprised him now, at any rate. There was no affectation in the tone of astonishment with which he re-echoed my words.

'Run away !' he exclaimed, staring at me.

'Run away. I should run away to England. I should give up everything here —my lessons, my career, my studies, all that I love in Rome—and I should go home without hesitation, *taking Lucy with me.*'

Monsignore rose from his chair and came towards me with an amiable and sympathizing expression of countenance.

'My dear child,' he said, ' do not distress yourself. I see you really are in earnest.' (I was then neither more nor less in earnest than I had been from the beginning of our interview.) 'I honour your affection for your sister and your almost maternal care of her. Lucia has told me how you have devoted yourself to her. You cannot seriously suppose that I wish to divide you from your sister. No, no ; rather would it be my fervent desire to bring you with her into the safe fold. But I tell you at once that I have never dissuaded Lucia from accompanying you to Tivoli. Her going or staying does not in the least depend upon me. How should it ?'

' Will you give me your authority to tell Lucy that you do not oppose her going ?'

' Certainly ! freely, gladly ! I believe it would be a very good thing for her. She looks a little thin and pale, don't you think so ? If she had asked my advice on the subject, I should at once have said " Go !" But she never said a word about it to me.'

' If you had been so kind as to tell me so sooner, Monsignore, I might have spared you much useless talking.'

' Don't think of that, don't think of that ! The truth is, I could hardly at first believe you serious in your little attack on me. I'm not a Macchiavelli nor a Jesuit after the model of Exeter Hall. Well, well, you will learn to know me better one day. Meanwhile, I admire your candour, I assure you. And don't distress yourself, my dear child, about being separated from your sister. We are not monsters, we poor priests, in spite of Exeter Hall, ha, ha, ha !'

I hurried away as quickly as I could, and went straight to the schoolroom to give Lucy the news. I did not believe Chiappaforti's statement that he had never opposed her visit to Tivoli. But at least he had distinctly consented to it now, and that was the chief thing with me. I burst into the schoolroom unceremoniously. Lucy looked up, startled to see me at that unaccustomed hour. But she was not more startled than I was when I saw Don Vittorio Corleoni seated beside her at the school-table.

CHAPTER VII.

Don Vittorio had receded into the dim background of my thoughts. I had satisfied myself that whatever admiration he had felt for Lucy was a mere passing fancy, and that he had soon grown tired of bringing English letters to the schoolroom to be translated. · And my mind had been too full of the subject of Lucy's conversion to have room for him. All the more was I startled and vexed to find him seated familiarly at my sister's elbow.

Lucy's face was covered with a deep,

sudden blush. Don Vittorio rose very calmly, and made me his usual formal bow, with his heels drawn together. The two little girls stared at me. No doubt I looked anything but a pleasant-humoured visitor; although the instant before, while my hand was still on the lock of the door, I had been cheerful enough—and even a little triumphant. Now my triumph was very effectually damped. I briefly and drily stated my object in coming to the schoolroom : namely, to tell Lucy that Monsignor Chiappaforti approved, and even advised, her going to Tivoli. And then I stood still, in an attitude of expectation.

That which I was waiting for soon happened. Don Vittorio took his departure, with another bow to me, a trifle haughtier than the first one. As he turned away, little Livia pulled him by the coat. 'Vit-

torio, Vittorio!' she cried, 'don't forget to
ask Laura for the ultramarine! And she
promised me some more gold-paper. Francesca has had twice as much as I.'

Livia was the youngest of the family, and
was supposed to enjoy the honour of being
her brother's favourite. He certainly permitted her to be more familiar and exigent
with him than any of the others, whom he
kept at a cool distance.

On this occasion he carelessly stroked the
child's hair, and answered, ' I have something
else to do, you monkey, than run on errands
all day between you and Laura. I am
going out now. I have brought you Laura's
message, and wasted five minutes in doing
so. You mustn't ask anything else of me for
a month.' And with that he went away.

He had brought Laura's message! Was
that the real reason for his presence in the

schoolroom, or a mere excuse? He had
certainly looked at me as he spoke, as who
should say, ' I hope you are satisfied as to
the reason of my being here?' And why
should that not be the simple truth? Was
I not growing morbid and suspicious, and
imbibing some of that universal mistrust
which poisoned the social atmosphere around
me, and which I had frequently proved to
be unfounded? No doubt I had shown my
chagrin and surprise very plainly in my face,
like a ' blunt barbarian,' as Signor Sandro
had called me. And no doubt Don Vittorio
had understood my emotion—it was entirely within the compass of his intelligence.
And having understood it, and being too
proud to offer anything like an explanation
to me, was it not natural that he should
take this indirect method of conveying to me
that he had no personal inclination to visit

the schoolroom, and that he considered his stay there to have been five minutes 'wasted'? Yes, certainly; very natural. And yet——

I was so absorbed in my own reflections that I scarcely comprehended the children's noisy and eager appeals to me, in their imperfect English, to look at the illuminations they had been doing, and to pronounce between gold and silver for the bordering of a bright scarlet letter B. I did comprehend, however, that Don Vittorio had really brought them a message from their elder sister—something concerning the all-important bazaar, of course—and further gathered that Don Vittorio had good-naturedly charged himself with the message, because I happened to be absent at my interview with Monsignore, and Donna Laura had no one else at hand. Nothing could be clearer or simpler. I was ashamed of myself for not feeling quite easy. But—I could not feel quite easy.

Lucy began to question me about Monsignor Chiappaforti :—What had he said to me? Was he not amiable and sweet-tempered? Why had I supposed he would object to her going to Tivoli? I was still absent-minded, and gave her short answers. When we were alone in our own lodging that evening I told her that Monsignore had declared that she (Lucy) had never consulted him at all about our projected holiday, nor had spoken to him on the subject.

'Neither did I,' she replied at once.

'You did *not?*'

'Certainly not. Why should you look so astounded? Did you suppose Monsignore was telling you a wilful and deliberate falsehood?'

I was obliged to confess that I had thought so, and to submit humbly to a lecture from my younger sister on the blindness of Protestant prejudice and the uncharitableness of Protestant judgments. It was impossible for me to doubt Lucy's sincerity. I must then conclude that it was not Monsignore's influence which had made her so reluctant to leave Rome.

'Then I suppose,' said I, 'it was the Princess Olympia who set herself so strongly against letting you go.'

'She does not like the children's lessons to be interrupted, as I told you, Catherine. And—and I think, myself, that we shall find it cold at Tivoli at this time of year.'

She had turned away her face from me as she spoke the last sentence, and dropped her voice timidly. I could not bear to see her seem afraid of me. There was nothing

I dreaded more than to make her shrink shyly from confiding all she thought and felt to me. And yet I had resolved to be perfectly candid and straightforward with her. My mind was painfully tossed backwards and forwards from one course of conduct to another. Monsignore had talked of my 'strength of mind'; and Lucy believed me to be quite terrible in my inflexible force of will. If they had but known how wavering and helpless I really felt! how much in need of courage and wisdom!

We went to Tivoli at the end of that week; but, oh, how different a visit it was from that to which I had so long looked forward! Lucy was — not sullen; that could not be, but—often sad. Monsignore's observation on her pale looks and thinness was a just one. She was looking almost painfully delicate. But I expected day by day to see the colour tinge her cheeks again, and the old gay light come into her eyes. I looked in vain. The sweet country air, the loveliness of the scenery, and the peaceful serenity of our outward lives, seemed to be vain medicaments for my Lucy's melancholy. And it was not alone that she was melancholy—she was secret, silent, strangely reserved with me. I had given my word not to discuss with her any question touching the Catholic creed during our absence from Rome, and therefore on that subject the lips of both of us were sealed. But in a hundred ways I felt that the old familiar confidence between us was at an end. Would it ever return? Just one year ago I had been looking out over the same wondrous landscape that lay now beneath my eyes—just one year, and how much was changed for me!

I had my Art still. Signor Sandro

would have grimly told me to be thankful, and mind nothing else. Other persons had talked to me in more high-flown terms, saying that Art was sufficient to the true artist; that the goddess would accept no half-hearted sacrifice; that one must cheerfully offer up all the human part of one's life to her, if need were—and the like tinkling phrases. But I could never cheat myself with words. All this talk, as if Art were some dim, monstrous abstraction served by creatures all hand and eye, and ignorant, from long disuse, of human sympathies, and weaknesses, and disgusts, and disappointments, seemed to me mere rhapsodical stuff. Perhaps, if I had been a genius, I might have found Art all-sufficient. (Although, to be honest, I doubt it; having noticed in all the accounts of men of genius with which I am acquainted that their sensitiveness to mundane troubles — even such vulgar ones as poor pay for their work, or hostile criticism of it—was in nowise blunted by the favour of the Muses.) At all events, not being a genius, nor anything near to one, I required several other things besides Art to make me happy. And yet I was not unthankful for those two good gifts of Heaven, Imagination and Labour. Nay, I had never valued them so highly as when I found in them a consolation for sorrow, and a refuge from care. To me they were both, at this time.

I worked hard at a study for the picture I had contemplated making, and for which I had found an admirable model. I also made several studies of landscape. One of these latter was at the ruins of the Villa of Quinctilius Varus, a mile or so from Tivoli. I used to walk thither in the early morning

with no other escort than a black-eyed bare-
footed urchin whom I had engaged to carry
my camp-stool and easel. Once or twice
Lucy had accompanied me, and we had eaten
our luncheon there, sitting under a gnarled
olive-tree, and looking over the matchless
panorama. But she found the walk too
fatiguing to make it frequently—what a
pang it gave me to hear her say so, and to
assure myself from anxious observation of
her languid gait and pale face that it was
but too true !—and so I spent many a morning there without her. She, meanwhile,
passed the time of my absence chiefly in the
Villa d'Este. There she was safe from in-
truders, and could wander about the grounds,
or sit still with her book or ~~her work~~ in the
shade. The old housekeeper at the Villa
d'Este was a great friend of mine, and used
to assure me, every time I gave her a small

present of money proportioned to my humble purse, that my sister was an angel, and that she (the housekeeper) would not fail to look after her. Let her come to the gardens as often and stay as long as she would! I do not know what more the good woman could have said, for ten times the money.

We had been at Tivoli about a week when one morning my little model came to me in a state of great excitement. She was a girl of fourteen, and looked, to English eyes, three or four years older; a handsome creature, with glorious eyes and rich masses of coarse, blue-black hair, but with a skin parched and sickly from fever, which she had suffered from severely. Her home was on the borders of the Pontine Marshes, in the very stronghold of malaria, and she had been sent to stay with a relative who lived in Tivoli, in order to regain her health. I had

heard of her from Signor Sandro, who had
often employed an elder sister of hers, a
professional model, in Rome. My little
Monica was not a professional model, but
she was just what I wanted for my picture,
fever-blanched skin and all. She looked
sad, pathetic, poetic ; but the charm vanished
the instant she opened her mouth to speak.
She had the harsh, hoarse, bawling voice
which belongs to so many Roman women of
her class, and the matter of her speech did
not compensate for its manner. She was
the most ignorant and undisciplined human
creature I had ever known ; but probably
she was not below the level of her compeers
in those respects. Such as her character
was, she revealed it as undisguisedly as any
wild animal. Her very lies—and she never
scrupled to utter one, if it suited her at the
moment—were of a wholly incredible and

inartificial kind ; and the detection of them embarrassed her not a whit, although it sometimes put her in a passion !

To me one morning came this unsophis ticated young person in a violent excitement, as I have said. She was even paler than usual, her black brows were bent into a frown, and she clenched her sunburnt fist, and kept muttering to herself in a fierce spasmodic way.

'This will not do, Monica,' said I. 'If you are so restless, and put on that demoniac look, you are not of the least use to me. Sit still, and leave off frowning.'

She shrugged her shoulders impatiently, but obeyed for a minute or so. Then the gesticulations and mutterings and general air of ferocity began again. I threw down my brush. 'Very well, Monica,' I said quietly, 'you are not disposed to earn your

money this morning, I see. As you please.
Only pray understand that I cannot afford to
pay you for wasting my time with your antics. .
I am not a rich Signora, but a poor artist.'

Monica jumped up, and kicked over the
stool on which she had been sitting, with a
violent imprecation. 'I care nothing for
your miserable money!' she cried. 'I *can't*
sit still! My blood is boiling in my
veins!'

'You are extremely silly, Monica. And
you don't speak the truth, either. You care
a great deal for my money.'

She paused in her furious tearing about
the room, and stared at me curiously. My
tone of cool indifference always had some
influence with her—simply, I believe, because it puzzled her. The violence of her
passion had not been affected, any more than
the passion of a little child is affected, whom

yet one can divert from its wrath and its screams by holding up any new object before its eyes. With Monica, as with the infant, there were no inner depths of the spirit to be profoundly stirred ; and consequently her storms of emotion were brief, and left no ground-swell behind them.

'Come,' said I, 'sit down there whilst I sketch in this background, and tell me what is the matter. Perhaps you will be able to be quiet when you have said your say.'

The idea seemed to please her. 'Yes, yes ; I will tell you. It will take a weight from my heart. Listen, Signorina !'

Monica's 'saying her say' involved so many rambling parentheses, so much violent language, and general incoherence, that I must condense her statement to me. It was this :

Some years previously her brother—much

older than she—had been sent to the galleys. He had had a narrow escape of being executed, indeed, for it was in the 'time of the priests,' as Monica phrased it, when malefactors used actually to be killed and made an end of. Not that Pasquale was a malefactor! By no means. He was an excellent young man, the pride of his family ; but he had had the misfortune to allow his feelings to get the better of him, and, in a word, he had attempted to murder a gentleman, and would have succeeded, but that his gun missed fire. And the gentleman had never rested until Pasquale was caged by the myrmidons of the law, declaring (with some reason, it should appear) that his life was not safe whilst that impetuous youth was at large.

At this point of her story Monica paused, expecting sympathy. I was obliged to disappoint her, and to explain that in my country we had a strong objection to assassins.

'Assassins!' she cried indignantly; 'but Pasquale was no assassin; it was a *vendetta!* A vengeance from jealousy—love jealousy.'

I could not say that this altered the case so as to make Pasquale an entirely admirable hero in my eyes; but I was curious to know how the gentleman (whom Monica described as a grand Signore, a great nobleman, rich, and proud, and splendid) could have been a rival to her brother, the peasant. She explained the matter without circumlocution. Pasquale had had a sweetheart whom he meant to marry some day. The sweetheart —a strikingly beautiful girl, according to Monica's account—had loved, or seemed to love, Pasquale, until one fine day her affections were captivated by the noble gentleman in question, who carried her off to

Rome with him, and after a short time abandoned her. Pasquale, who had been for some weeks deceived and hoodwinked, both by his faithless *innamorata* and her seducer, no sooner discovered the truth than he tried to kill the nobleman. What could be more natural? And then Pasquale— *poveretto*—had been hunted for days and days by the *giandarmi* (gendarmes), and caught at last, and sent to the galleys. What a pity that he had not sent a bullet into the traitor's heart first! That would have been some consolation under the suffering of imprisonment : but, as it was, Pasquale's case was really too hard, and calculated to awaken the deepest sympathy !

Such was Monica's story, and such her view of it.

And what, I asked, had become of Pasquale ? Oh, he had escaped from the

galleys after about a year and a half. But
as to what he had been doing since, or where
he had been, Monica either could not, or
would not, give any information. He had
been 'in the Abruzzi,' she said vaguely.
Indeed, she believed he had crossed the sea
to Sicily. She did not know where Sicily
was, but it was a long, long way off. You
see, Pasquale could not come home to his
old place, because the accursed police would
put him in prison again if they caught him.
Poor Pasquale !

And the girl whom he had loved ? Oh,
about her Monica knew nothing. And the
fine nobleman ? Ah, *he*, the traitor, the
wretch, the miscreant, who had set on the
giandarmi to hunt down poor Pasquale and
put him in prison, he was alive, he was
flourishing, he was brave with sleek clothes
and a gold chain, and a horse that shone

like satin ! She (Monica) had seen him that very morning in Tivoli, as she crossed the Piazza. She was but nine years old when poor Pasquale had the misfortune to attempt his murder, but she remembered his face well— well. Might he die assassinated !

'Then it was the sight of this gentleman that put you into such a ferment?' I said.

Truly it was. What else? But now she had spoken, her heart was lighter. She felt easier. But she did not want to see that villain again. The sight of him caused her to 'make bad blood.' And what could she do? Pasquale was away, no one knew where. She could only hope and pray that the saints would pour down evils and misfortunes on the head of that traitor, for he seemed to be beyond the reach of earthly vengeance— more was the pity !

I mused over this story and the strange scene of Monica's violence as I walked down, a little later, to the Villa d'Este to meet Lucy, and bring her home to dinner. ' What a curious savage the girl is !' thought I. And then I began to consider her from a professional point of view, and to think of making a study of her face in its unrestrained fury, and calling it ' Vendetta !' It might not, however, be easy to bring her passion, on that score, up to the boiling point again. ' And even if I could do it,' I said to myself, ' the experiment would be something like irritating a vigorous young tiger, with the view of studying him in his wrath. There's no reckoning on what she might do !'

Lucy met me near the gate of the gardens, and to my surprise I found she was not alone. She was in company with an elderly

priest, who took off his great shovel hat and
saluted me with much politeness.

'This gentleman—Don Gregorio Galli,'
said Lucy, 'is a friend of the Princess
Corleoni's. When he heard that we knew
the Princess, he was kind enough to offer
to be of service to us here.'

'In any way—in any way in my power,
Signorina,' said Don Gregorio. 'You are
strangers in Tivoli. Pray let me know if I
can give you help or information of any kind.
And how was Monsignor Chiappaforti when
you left Rome? A man of very distinguished talent—a shining light. Ah,
Rome is his true sphere! There his abilities
are appreciated. At one time there was a
chance of my getting a parish in Rome
myself, but circumstances have kept me here.
Well, well, we must try to do our duty in
our humble way. I shall do myself the

pleasure to come and see you, Signorina; meanwhile I have the honour to salute you.'

Then Don Gregorio walked off one way, whilst we pursued the other. He was a meagre, feeble-looking old man, with a weak, self-complacent countenance. I have seldom conversed with anyone so dirty, or more urbane.

I was put out by his intrusion into our life, although I believed he was not to blame for it. I thought that I was unfairly used in having to submit to Don Gregorio's visits, which were made of course with the sole view of Lucy's conversion, whilst, on my side, I had faithfully kept my word, and refrained from trying to influence my sister's mind on the subject of religion. This vexed me, and I spoke out what I thought of it, and Lucy protested her belief that Don

Gregorio merely came to see us out of pure benevolence and humanity, apart from all thoughts of proselytizing ; and the discussion drove Monica and her story out of my head for the rest of that day.

CHAPTER VIII.

A POISONED SHAFT.

FROM that day we were haunted by Don Gregorio. Even Lucy found his frequent company oppressive, although she would hardly acknowledge as much openly. As for me, I daily threatened to affront him past forgiveness, and so get rid of his visits, and daily found it impossible to carry out the threat ; so mild, long-suffering, and impervious to the broadest hints did I find his reverence. 'If he would but wash his hands *sometimes!*' I exclaimed in despair. And indeed his divorce from soap and water

was not the least of the disturbances to my
peace of mind occasioned by Don Gregorio's
presence. I wondered at first why Monsignor Chiappaforti, who was certainly a
shrewd, clever man, had entrusted any
mission of conversion to Don Gregorio Galli:
since even Lucy's charitable judgment could
not but rate him low in intelligence, and
even Lucy's humility must find it difficult
not to look down upon, instead of up to
him. But it soon became clear to me that
Don Gregorio was employed not to guide
my young sister, but to watch her. And
Monsignore had shown his usual acuteness
in selecting him for this task. The Signor
Curato's zeal was indefatigable, and his good
temper (or stupidity) impregnable. Go
where we might, do what we would, many
hours of the day did not pass without our
seeing the rusty black suit and dusty shovel

hat of Don Gregorio, and hearing his long-
winded complimentary speeches, the utter
fatuity, formality, and falseness of which
had an absolutely paralyzing effect on me. I
used to sit dumbly staring at his reverence's
unwashed and unshaven countenance, and
listening to his reverence's soul-exhausting
commonplaces, with the helpless sensation
of a sleeper oppressed by nightmare.

One refuge I had from him, or I believe
his persecution would have driven me from
Tivoli : I could get away from him to the
Villa of Quinctilius, and paint in peace. That
was rather too long an excursion for Don
Gregorio. Perhaps, indeed, he might even
have got out so far as that in pursuit of
Lucy ; but it was not worth his while to
follow me thither. Lucy, meanwhile,
passed her mornings safely in the gardens
of the Villa d'Este ; and though the old

priest occasionally looked in upon her even there, he seemed to be satisfied to leave her for the most part in the seclusion and almost solitude of the gardens. At that time of year visitors were few, and if a stray party of tourists did appear, it was easy to avoid them.

Meanwhile, I was working earnestly, sometimes at the landscape, and sometimes at the study of Monica's head. That volcanic young person was now in a period of quiescence. She had had a slight return of the intermittent fever. This had subdued her, and she would now sit still for hours, in a languid, restful attitude, which was the very thing I wanted, so that I got on famously, and began to hope that I should make a fairly good thing of my picture. The picture itself was not properly begun; but I meant to work at it when I returned to Rome, under my master's eye. What I was doing in Tivoli was merely to make studies for it. My notion was to paint a kind of personification of the wild, sad, fever-stricken, mournfully beautiful Roman Campagna, under the form of a female peasant, and to call it 'A Child of the Soil,' or some such name. For this purpose, Monica seemed to me a perfect model; especially when her natural savagery was only smouldering, as it were, beneath the languor of laziness and malaria. Her tiger flashes of ferocity (however interesting a study in themselves) were not for my present purpose. I therefore refrained from recurring to the subject of her enemy, the nobleman. And she seemed to have thought no more of him since the day when his unexpected appearance in Tivoli had so moved her. During some happy interval

of release from the society of Don Gregorio,
I began to give a brief outline of Monica's
story to Lucy. But I almost regretted
having done so when I saw what an impression it made on my sister. She was even
uneasy at my spending hours alone with such
a fierce, untamed creature.

'Her brother, you know, was a murderer
in intent, Catherine,' said Lucy, with a
shudder; 'and I fear she would not scruple
to follow his example, if she were provoked.'

I tried to laugh my sister out of her
tremors. 'I believe I am safe from assassin-
ation,' said I, 'unless, indeed, I expire of
exhaustion after a long visit from Don
Gregorio.' But I was rather glad that I
had not mentioned the fact of Pasquale's
rival having actually been seen in Tivoli,
and that Lucy had interrupted me before I
had got to that point; for she was so ner-

vous and horror-stricken at my account of
Monica's code of ethics that, if she had
known this circumstance, she would have
been tormented by the apprehension of some
scene of violence and bloodshed. Always
timid and gentle, she had of late become
nervous to excess. Her spirits and health
were evidently being undermined by a con-
stant anxiety and mental struggle. Sometimes, when I looked at her, I was tempted
to wish that she would make the final resolve,
and openly become a Catholic. Anything
would be better than this doubt and suspense.
Again, the project would cross my mind to
give up all my studies in Rome, and return
with Lucy to England, as I had threatened
Monsignore I would do. In that case, fare-
well to all hope of future distinction and
present improvement in my art. But that
hope—although it was dear to me—I would

unhesitatingly have sacrificed, if by so doing I could ensure my sister's peace of mind. Yes ; I am sure, on calmly looking back to that time, that I would have made the sacrifice. Nor do I deem it a great boast to say so. To see Lucy anxious and unhappy poisoned all my life ; and no artistic glories I could conceive of would have had power to elate me whilst she was depressed.

I come now to a strange crisis in our lives, which seemed to overtake us as suddenly as an Alpine storm ; but which had, of course, been gradually prepared by many circumstances working blindly together ; and by some other circumstances artfully arranged and combined to one end. The first shock of it came in this form :

Lucy one evening received a letter sealed with a large coat-of-arms. Our correspondents were very few, and none of them,

I need scarcely say, used such aristocratic signs of dignity as the ostentatious heraldic device in red wax which made Lucy's letter look imposing. I handed it to her with a jest about her grand correspondent. She took it with a smile, which grew brighter when she had cast her eyes on the superscription. 'It is the Princess's writing,' she said. 'Very likely there is a letter inside from Francesca and Livia. They were to be allowed to write to me, if they could manage to achieve an epistle in English.'

She broke the seal, still smiling, and I went on with some needlework that I had in hand. 'Well,' said I, after some minutes' silence, 'is the children's English undecipherable?' and at the same time I lifted my eyes from my stitching. What I saw forced a cry of terror from me. Lucy sat

there pale to the lips, with the open letter
on the table before her, and a look of such
frozen anguish on her white face as almost
made my heart stand still!

'My Lucy!' I cried, 'my child! what is
the matter?'

She shivered, and trembled violently from
head to foot, but did not speak.   When I
grasped at the letter, she feebly tried to
hold it back, with a little piteous moan; but
I seized it without scruple.   And I read it
whilst she sat cowering and trembling in her
chair, with her face hidden in her clasped
hands.

Oh, it was a cruel letter!   The Princess Olympia—for she was the writer—
thoroughly understood the softness and
sensibility of the nature she was minded to
wound.   Not a word was lost; not a sting
was mitigated by one touch of pity.   The

Princess began at once by a direct accusation :

'You have repaid my kindness by black ingratitude,' she wrote. 'You have tried to seduce my son away from me, from his duty, and from his station. Your arts appear the more hateful from being cloaked under an appearance of modest simplicity. My innocent children have revealed to me the frequent interviews which they witnessed between Don Vittorio and yourself. I am loath to sully their pure minds with such suspicions as attach to your conduct, but it will be my imperative duty to warn them against you, and to forbid them to see you, or communicate with you in any way. How far your insolent sister has been your accomplice, I know not. She is an unscrupulous and irreligious woman, the companion of revolutionary infidels, and her conduct, therefore, is not surprising. But in *you* I have been grossly deceived. The dreadful suspicion assails me that your desire to be instructed in our holy faith was merely a part of your plan to ingratiate yourself with my family for the basest purposes. But this idea is so truly horrible, that I fervently pray it may be erroneous. Attempt not any exculpation. It would be in vain. I know all. My son followed you to Tivoli. He has had stolen interviews with you there in the gardens of the Villa d'Este. Your reputation is destroyed for ever, if I speak one half of what I know and can prove against you. Your sister's professional career in Rome can be cut short by a word from me. What decent, self-respecting persons, even among the heretics, would countenance such dangerous and wily women, when once unmasked?

'But I would not shut the door against repentance. Heaven forbid! Repent, amend, do penance in the dust! Seek out some holy guide to the true religion. Implore the compassion of the Blessed Virgin for the evil past, and her strengthening help for the future. It is your only hope.

'OLYMPIA BASTIANI CORLEONI.

'Indulge in no self-delusions. Vittorio has confessed everything to me.

'O. B. C.'

This was to me so utterly unexpected, that I know not whether amazement or burning indignation were the greater as I read. But the amazement passed, and the indignation remained—and remains. But for the moment my sole care was for Lucy. All other feelings were forcibly thrust aside by anxiety for her. I cannot describe the strange state of prostration she had fallen into. She was like one who has received a stunning blow, in the literal sense of the words. A sort of numbness seemed to have taken possession of all her faculties. It seemed a painful effort for her even to articulate a word in answer to my attempts to soothe and comfort her. She did not lament, she did not shed a tear, but just sat still in her chair, ashy pale, and shivering from head to foot like a terrified bird. I was terrified in my turn. This state of nervous prostration was something of which I had no experience, and I knew not how to deal with it. I touched Lucy's hand; it was cold and listless. I spoke to her again and again ; she merely shook her head feebly, and cowered away from me in her chair with a shrinking movement of the shoulders. What was to be done? She could not be allowed to remain thus.

In the midst of my most painful perplexity, the landlady of the humble lodging came into the room to announce a visit from Don Gregorio.

'Send him away,' said I ; 'my sister is ill.'

The woman, who, though coarse and ignorant, was kindly, and, like most of her countrywomen, intensely sympathetic with illness, advanced to see what was the matter. Her experience suggested but one cause for Lucy's trembling. 'She shivers,' said the Signora Anna, commonly called 'S'ora Nanna ;' 'she has the fever. Oh! it will be nothing, Signorina. Don't take on. Get her to bed, and cover her up warm and

give her a dose of quinine. By-and-by the
hot fit will come on.'

The suggestion was welcome to me,
because, although I did not believe Lucy
had fever—or at least not the malaria fever
which the S'ora Nanna meant—yet it was
evident that she was ill; and this notion of
the fever furnished an excuse for having her
nursed and kept quiet, which would be
accepted without question. And I could
not say aloud, ' My sister has been poisoned
by venomous words.' We must keep that
to ourselves for awhile. She submitted to
go to bed. She let me undress her and
cover her up with cloaks and shawls. I
made her a warm drink, and though she
piteously begged to be left quiet, she submitted to swallow it without much difficulty,
and then lay down with her face hidden in
the pillow, and her bright curls tossed in

disorder about it. After a little hesitation I resolved to leave her for half an hour or so in the hope that she might fall asleep from pure exhaustion. 'Pray God that wicked woman has not murdered her!' I exclaimed aloud in the misery of my heart as I closed the bedroom door.

In the sitting-room, standing at the window and looking out into the tangled wilderness of weeds and shrubs that they called a garden, I found Don Gregorio. The brief twilight was coming on rapidly, and he loomed large and black in it against the window-panes. My entrance into the room caused him to turn round.

'Ah, Signorina,' he began, with his usual flourishing bow, 'I am so grieved to hear of your dear sister's illness. I trust it is not serious; I——'

'You had better go away,' said I. 'I cannot talk to you now—nor listen.'

'Certainly not, Signorina. You cannot be expected to listen, I am sure. I am *so* sorry to hear of the Signorina Lucia's illness! Just at this time, too, when I am expecting the great pleasure and honour of a visit from Monsignor Chiappaforti. He arrives to-morrow; and he will make a point, I have no doubt, of coming to see our amiable invalid as soon as——'

I turned on him, being fairly at bay. 'He shall not come here to torment my sister,' I said. 'I will not have her troubled or disturbed, for the Pope himself. Do you understand me? And now be so good as to take your departure. Go away. I think I speak plainly.'

My words, or my tone, or my stern, angry face, or all three together, succeeded in piercing Don Gregorio's suave dulness for once, at all events. He started, stared, backed a few steps from me, and then absolutely turned round and ran away, shuffling down the stairs as fast as his meagre old legs could carry him.

CHAPTER IX.

SERPENT AND DOVE.

My sister at length fell into a deep sleep, and I sat down to think at my leisure. First I read over again more than once the Princess's letter. In spite of the passion of indignation which surged up in me each time my eyes rested on its hateful words, I forced myself to read it attentively until I had thoroughly mastered its contents. Ugh! Even to think of it now makes me hot with anger, and at the time I believe it would have cost me a less effort of will to hold my hand against a scorching flame than it did to compel my mind steadily to consider that letter with all the judgment I could bring to bear on it.

First of all, there needed but little reflection to convince me that the Princess's statement respecting the 'revelations' made to her by the little girls, Francesca and Livia, of Don Vittorio's interviews with Lucy in the schoolroom, was a lying pretence. She ignorant of what went on day after day in her own house! I believe a mouse could hardly stir behind the wainscot but she knew it. No; had she wished to prevent her son's visits to the schoolroom she could have done so with perfect ease. Why she had chosen to permit those visits, and why, having permitted them, she now chose to reproach Lucy with them, I did not yet see.

The next point was a more startling and

painful one.   She spoke of stolen interviews
between her son and my sister in the gardens
of the Villa d'Este.   This, too, I was at
first convinced was a falsehood, but on a
second and calmer perusal of the letter that
conviction was shaken.   I could not waken
Lucy to question her then ; it would have
been too cruel.   And so the doubt remained
in my mind, as painful and irritating as a
thorn in the flesh.   But I must perforce
wait until next morning to remove it.

Thirdly, I was struck by the loophole
which the Princess left open to Lucy for a
possible reconciliation.   It is true she never
used that word.   She even declared that she
must forbid her children to hold any com-
munication with Lucy, or to see her again.
But I understood her phraseology well
enough to be sure that she intended to hold
out a glimmer of hope.   Her words about

cutting short my career in Rome; her phrase, 'Your reputation is destroyed for ever if I speak one half of what I know and can prove against you,' were all conditional threats. On what was their fulfilment, or non-fulfilment, to be contingent? Not on the Christian charity of Donna Olympia Corleoni, let the condition be what else it might. Heaven help any creature in her power who should depend on that hollow mockery! Her object seemed to me to be first to beat down Lucy into the dust, and then to raise her from it after her own good will and pleasure. She had reckoned on Lucy's childish inexperience, on her softness and timidity, on the sensitiveness of her affections. She had learned accurately the points of the girl's nature that could be most effectually hurt.

'But you have not quite as accurately

learned to know *me*, Donna Olympia Bastiani Corleoni !' I exclaimed to myself.

Lucy still slept, or seemed to sleep, when I went to my bed beside hers in the same room. The next morning I awoke with the dawn, and looking over at her, saw her pale face tinted with the rose-hues of sunrise, and the tears stealing down her cheeks from beneath her closed eyelids. I arose, and wrapped some clothes loosely round me, and went and seated myself on the side of her bed.

'Lucy,' I said, 'you are not sleeping. I want to talk to you.'

She shrank away, hiding her face in the pillow without opening her eyes, and murmured brokenly :

'Oh, Catherine, don't be angry with me ! Don't *you* cease to love me, or I shall die !'

'Angry with you, my pet ! No, little

Lucy, my little sister that I have loved from a tiny, tiny infant ! You cannot think that I shall cease to love you. If your dear dead mother could come back to earth, I think even she would be content with my love for you, Lucy.'

Then the poor child burst into a passion of sobbing, and throwing her arms round my neck, blessed and thanked me and begged me to forgive her and love her still, though she had been ' very, very wrong to deceive me,' until my eyes filled too, and we cried in each other's arms. The ebullition of her pent-up feelings relieved her heart, over-charged with sorrow and shame and vague terrors. And presently she was able to speak to me clearly and with something like calmness. The gist of what she told me was this :

Don Vittorio Corleoni had professed the

most fervent love for her. The first announcement of his passion had been made in a little note slipped into her hand with the English letter she was to translate. In it he had conjured her to keep his secret for the present, as he should have to encounter many troubles and annoyances if it were known as yet. He trusted to her honour not to betray him to his mother, or to her sister, or to anyone. She had returned his note to him at the earliest opportunity, and had told him that if he so addressed her again she should be compelled to appeal to the Princess. So far, so good. But what chance had little soft-hearted, simple-minded Lucy against Vittorio Corleoni? The poor child had fallen in love with the fine qualities her romantic fancy attributed to that handsome, high-bred mask, those beautiful deep blue eyes. I have recently read somewhere the dictum enunciated by a masculine critic that ' no man but a fool can fail to perceive when a woman is in love with him.' Don Vittorio's folly, at all events, was not of the kind which is apt to fall into mistakes from diffidence of his own attractions or a too exalted opinion of the claims of others. He thought it the most probable thing in the world that Lucy should be in love with him; any other state of things would have been almost inconceivable to him.

In a word, he persuaded her to trust in him, and to keep the first secret she had ever had from me. It is not a new or rare case. A sister, even the fondest, has small chance against a lover, when they are weighed by a girl of eighteen in all the enchantment of a first romance of the heart. But Lucy vowed—and I believed her—that her secrecy from me was to be only for a

brief while ; that she never ceased to urge
Vittorio to confide in me, whom she could
trust as herself, she assured him ; and that
he constantly promised to tell me everything
soon if Lucy would but be patient and
prudent for a little time. He had even
spoken of his great respect for me and admiration of my talents, and had hinted at the
great things he and Lucy might be able to
do for my advancement as an artist. Ah,
poor, credulous, unsuspecting child ! He
had fooled her to the top of her bent. The
extent of his influence over her was more
startlingly represented to me by the following circumstance than by anything else :
She had kept the most absolute silence about
his pursuit of her, even to Monsignor
Chiappaforti ! That that astute gentleman
more than suspected it I did not doubt,
but at least he had not heard a hint of

it from Lucy. She had been firm and staunch.

The efforts to convert her had gone on in the Palazzo Corleoni simultaneously with Don Vittorio's wooing, but apart from it. Lucy, poor child, was eager to assure me that her mind had been drawn to the Roman Catholic Church before she had ever thought of Vittorio as a lover. And I did not doubt that she spoke the truth. Nevertheless, I did not doubt also that — unconsciously, perhaps, to herself—her infatuation for Don Vittorio prepared her to be infatuated with his faith, with his family, with his country, with all that belonged to him. By a series of searching questions I gathered from Lucy that Don Vittorio had shown himself but lukewarm on the subject of her conversion. And this fact alone would have been suf- ficient to convince me (even had there not been, alas! a crowd of others pointing to the same conclusion) that he did not mean honourably by her. His wife—the wife of Don Vittorio de' Principi Bastiani Corleoni and the future head of the house!—must of course belong to the true Church. Heresy would have meant degradation, decadence, social ostracism for his wife; but for his mistress, the case was different. My blood boiled in my veins as I thought of it all. But no suspicion of this kind appeared to have crossed Lucy's mind. Having once begun her confession, she spoke freely and without reservation.

'Vittorio cannot blame me for telling you now,' she said.

She even showed me the precious scrap of paper in which he had first declared his love—I loathe to profane that word in writing of him—but although neither in

that, nor in any of his reported utterances
to her did the word 'marriage' once occur,
she never appeared to doubt for an instant
that he sought her as his wife. Distantly
and cautiously, I ventured to hint a suspicion; but I need not have feared to startle
her. Her mind seemed incapable of taking
in such an idea. Her only conception of
my meaning was that I accused her lover of
possible weakness in yielding to the opposition of his family, and so giving her up.
And to this she merely replied, with a
trembling lip and tearful eyes: 'I know I
am far beneath him in every way, and I
would not be an obstacle in his path, or a
clog on him—only I do believe that no one
else would make him so happy as I, because
no one else *could* love him as I love him.'

It was maddening to hear her talk so.
And, although I put a strong constraint on

myself, being resolved to be gentle and patient with her, I could not help my voice taking a sterner tone as I asked the direct question: 'Lucy, does the Princess speak falsely when she says you have had stolen interviews with her son in the gardens of the Villa d'Este?'

'No; she speaks truly—at least, as she thinks, truly. I was going to tell you how it was, Catherine. Vittorio came here without my knowledge. We had had a little quarrel—at least, he had been vexed at my coming to Tivoli. When you thought Monsignore was setting himself against the visit you were mistaken. It was really Vittorio. But he ought not to be blamed for that. He only wanted to keep me in Rome because he was fond of me, you know.'

'Or of himself! Well, go on.'

'But then, when I was gone, he was so

miserable. He wanted to write to me, but then he thought you—might——'

' Well ?'

' He knew you would see the letter, and perhaps question me about it, and so—he resolved to ride over all the way, only on the chance of being able to catch a glimpse of me, even if he could not speak to me. He would not have done that, Catherine, if he had not loved me truly.'

' And was it his true love which induced him to follow you to the gardens of the Villa when you were alone ? He must have bribed the portress to let him in !'

' No, no, Catherine ! Indeed not ! She knew him. The Princess spent a summer once at Tivoli.'

' He then knowingly exposed you to the comments of that ignorant woman, full of the ideas and prejudices of her country, who of all the matter only knows that you are the sister of a poor artist, a young motherless girl, who receives stolen visits from a gentleman of Don Vittorio's rank and consequence! You see what his lady mother writes; how *she* views (or affects to view) such imprudent behaviour! Don Vittorio knows as well as the Princess that he was cruelly injuring your reputation in the eyes of all his people.'

But it was all of no use. She blamed herself, she was willing to humble herself to the dust; but Vittorio was noble-hearted, generous, magnanimous, a mirror of chivalry! How, then, did she interpret the Princess's words: 'My son has confessed everything,' and the Princess's scornful reproaches following thereon? Had not Don Vittorio betrayed his love's confidence, and given her up to insult and evil repute? If he could not control or mitigate the arrogant violence of his mother's resentment, he could at least have disowned it! He could have come and stood by Lucy openly—he could have written!

All in vain! I urged and urged in vain. And it grieved me to the soul to think how sharp the pain would be, how crushing the blow, when Lucy should be convinced by bitter experience that this idol she now worshipped was a poor, hollow, brittle, painted piece of clay.

The rest of that day passed miserably enough. Lucy was really ill; nervous, languid, and unable to take food. Towards four o'clock a violent headache oppressed her, and I made her go to bed, and darkened the windows; for the light hurt her poor eyes, inflamed with crying. Lucy had, apparently, not thought of making any reply

to the Princess Olympia's letter.   But I had
thought of it.   I would do nothing rashly,
but I had thought—not whether I should
answer the letter, for on that I was un-
shakably resolved—but how to answer it.
And I was still thinking, when I heard the
door of our sitting-room softly opened, and
a light footstep on the bare brick floor.
The step was very unlike S'ora Nanna's ox-
like tread.   I turned my head, and saw
Monsignor Chiappaforti.

CHAPTER X.

HE came forward with a sweet sympathizing look on his face—a look that needed but the slightest modification to serve for various occasions of condolence, from a broken tea-cup and genteel comedy, up to a broken heart and unfashionable tragedy. To which category he was disposed to assign my present troubles I was uncertain. I think he was himself uncertain for a few seconds. When he spoke it was in a moderate and measured tone of sympathy, and his countenance was just a very little less sweet, as

soon as he fully saw mine, than it had been
on his first entrance. 'This is a sad disappointment, my dear Signorina,' he said.
'I arrived here hoping to find both you and
our dear Lucia well and merry, and enjoying
your holiday, and now Don Gregorio tells
me that your sister is ill.'

'Yes, Monsignore ; she is ill.'

'Dear, dear, dear! What is it? A
touch of fever? Have you any advice for
her ?'

'I shall see that she is taken care of.'

'I am sure you will. There can be no
doubt of that.'

I had risen from my seat when I saw
him, and remained standing, he also standing,
with his large ecclesiastical hat in his hand.
I was vividly conscious of the contrast
between my curt roughness of speech and
manner and his smooth politeness ; but I

was resolved to make no pretences, nor to cry 'peace' with my lips when there was war in my heart. I did not doubt that Monsignore was privy to the fact of the Princess's cruel letter. Perhaps he had even inspired it. Of this at least I was sure, that all his feelings in the matter would be ranged on her side and against us.

'I hope my worthy friend Don Gregorio Galli has been able to be of some use to you here?' said Monsignore, with an amiable inflection of voice, which was so strongly contrasted with the tone of mine as to be almost ludicrous.

'No doubt he meant well, but I cannot say he has been of any use to us, Monsignore.'

'Ha, ha, ha! No, eh? Poor Don Gregorio! He is a good creature—a worthy soul—but he has lived remote from

the world and lacks *savoir vivre*, I dare
say, ha, ha, ha !'

'Monsignor Chiappaforti, you must forgive me if I speak abruptly. My sister is
ill. I am uneasy and troubled, and I
cannot now talk with you on indifferent
topics.'

The expression of his face changed at
once and completely, from smiling non-
chalance to steady gravity. He sat down,
put his hat on the table, and settling himself in his chair, said : 'Good. I understand. Will you talk on a topic which is
not indifferent ? Will you talk on a topic
which concerns Lucia ?'

'I cannot tell. I will not promise to
talk. But if you wish it, I will listen.'

Monsignore shrugged his shoulders very
slightly, and replied : 'That is something !
One must be thankful for the smallest con-

cession from so—ahem !—admirably resolute
a person.'

I made no answer, but folded my hands
on the table before me and waited.

'The fact is, that the Princess Corleoni
is displeased with Lucia ; very seriously displeased. This grieves me, I assure you.'

Here he paused, expecting me to speak,
but as I did not, he proceeded in the same
even, grave tone : 'Now you love frankness,
and have strength of mind to bear it ; therefore I will say frankly that I think Lucia
has been to blame. Frankly now, do you
not think so yourself?'

'Monsignore, to answer such a question
as that, made no part of my agreement with
you when I told you I would listen. However, before I could answer it, if I would, I
must know precisely what you mean in
asking it. To what point in my sister's

conduct do you refer? I take it for granted that you have some special thing in your mind for which you blame Lucy.'

'Has not the Princess written to her?' he asked, taken a little off his guard.

'The Princess has written to her.'

'Oh!'

He leant back in his chair, half closing his eyes and nodding to himself as if he were meditating my reply. In reality I believe he felt himself checked by my stubborn inflexibility. I think he had reckoned on being able to lead me on to talk, and then to guide my talking, as he was accustomed to guide most persons, into the direction he wished; using either a silken thread or a leathern thong, coaxing, urging, or restraining, as the case might require.

But my wrath burnt too hot within

me for such arts to avail. In truth, the
power of cunning — call it diplomacy, or
what other polite name you will—seems to
me to be greatly overrated. In general, it
weaves only cobweb meshes which are
shattered at the first stirring of any strong
and genuine feeling. Passion ignores and
overrides the 'laws of the game,' hacks
artful knots suddenly in two, and flings
a fierce sword into the nicely-balanced
scale.

I think Monsignor Giacomo Chiappaforti
scarcely made sufficient account of strong
and genuine feeling in his dealings with the
world. In the present case, instead of
saying to me, 'You are very indignant,' he
said, 'You are very cautious, Signorina.'
And I suppose he really credited me with
some deep scheme.

'However,' he proceeded, 'my duty, and

my strong feeling of interest in your sister,
alike command me to try to serve you. If
I am misunderstood——patience!'

'Monsignore, it is very easy to be understood, I think. One has only to speak the
truth plainly.'

'Alas! How often is the truth rejected
and misinterpreted! The head alone will
not suffice to receive it; it must be accepted
by the heart. Intellect, my dear young
lady, is no all-sufficient guide of conduct.
But as to Lucia—you say the Princess *has*
written to her?'

'And you say so too, Monsignore.'

'Ahem!—yes; I thought it likely, from
what she said to me, that she would write.
The Princess was much agitated. I trust
she did not write—ahem!—a—a—intemperately?'

'She wrote very intemperately.'

'Ah! Dear, dear, dear, I feared so! But you must make allowance for the feelings of a mother. The Princess is a devoted mother ; — an exemplary mother. When the maternal feelings are aroused, women do not stop to calculate or measure their words. We must have charity for the imperfections of human nature.'

'Monsignore, do you bring any message from the Princess Corleoni ?'

The thought had suddenly struck me that he had been sent to negotiate a reconciliation with Lucy.

'A message ? No ; oh no ! The Princess was too—too excited, when I saw her last, to think of sending a message to your sister. No ; my visit to you is prompted by other motives. Ahem ! You must be aware— since you tell me the Princess has written, and written in anger — that what has occurred places Lucia in a very sad and painful position.'

'Insult is certainly painful. And Lucy is exceptionally sensitive.'

'Ah! yes; but the matter is more serious than that. The Princess Corleoni is a very illustrious and influential lady. Her countenance and friendship can do much in Rome; and—naturally—her disapproval, on the other hand, carries with it a certain sort of social stigma. Now Lucia, I grieve to say it, has incurred her disapproval. I make allowances for your English habits of thought, and so forth; but still, not even in England, I believe, would it be considered venial for a young woman in Lucia's position to encourage the clandestine addresses of her employer's son! More particularly when that employer was of a rank so immeasurably superior to her own. You follow me?'

'You speak the language of the world, Monsignore ; but at least you speak explicitly, and of course I understand you.'

'You have nothing to oppose to what I say, Signorina ?'

'I do not think I am called on to enter into any defence of my sister to you, Monsignor Chiappaforti.'

'You will, at all events, be called on to undertake her defence to your own friends, to the world you live in, to society ! Social laws must be obeyed by those who wish to profit by their protection.'

'I renounce with contempt the "protection" of social laws which bully the weak and cringe to the strong. I despise from my soul the attempt to make mere compromises with the world, the flesh, and the devil, binding on my conscience as if they were divine institutions.'

My anger had flashed out in spite of me, like a sudden tongue of flame from a smouldering fire. The priest looked at me with a new expression of surprise on his face, mingled with sour aversion.

'These are strange sentiments, Signorina,' he said. 'I warn you that they are dangerous sentiments. I gave you credit for more sober sense than to be led away by such revolutionary notions. I had hoped that you would not encourage Lucia in conduct which gives such pain to her benefactress, and can only bring misery on herself. *You*, at least, must be convinced that Don Vittorio Corleoni can never marry your sister. It is too absurd an idea to be seriously entertained for a moment. The alternative, if she does not discourage his pursuit, is one which I suppose you are hardly prepared to accept, notwithstanding your disdain for the laws of society !'

At that moment I had a glimpse, not often vouchsafed to the profane vulgar, of the real Giacomo Chiappaforti, instead of the smooth, smiling, soft-voiced prelate, whose *bonhomie* and infantine gaiety of manner were so lauded and admired. And let me give Monsignore all the benefit to be obtained from the confession that, to me, the reality was preferable to the sham. The sham had disgusted and wearied me with its perpetual smile, its ready laugh from the teeth outward, its smooth, yet resolute ignoring of rough realities which were hurting other folks.

But now at last the real Giacomo Chiappaforti showed that he could be in earnest on occasion. His mouth was drawn into an expression of the bitterest sarcasm, his eyes glittered angrily, his very voice was changed, and had a hard metallic sound. This man was at least human enough to hate, it seemed.

'Then, Monsignore,' I said, disregarding his sneer against myself, 'you judge Don Vittorio Corleoni capable of dishonourably pursuing an innocent, motherless girl, a stranger, beneath *his* mother's roof? The Princess judges as you judge, and yet neither of you have anathemas for him! The "social laws" which Lucy is to obey on pain of losing their valuable protection have no protection to give her, nor any terrors for the man who would injure her! The morality which is revolted by Lucy's wickedness in believing a cruel lie, holds a sweetly charitable estimate of the liar.'

'Tut, tut!' exclaimed Chiappaforti, shrugging his shoulders, and fixing his mouth into a hard, cynical smile—'tut, tut, tut! This is the kind of high-flown sentimentality which might serve to excuse any offence, or crime, or blunder ; and very often does, I believe, amongst the philanthropic worshippers of revolution and irreligion. As to Lucia, I am willing to give her credit for innocence of intention at the beginning— youthful vanity is a great temptation, and hoodwinks the conscience. But the world will not judge so leniently. The world will say—unless the Princess can be induced to keep this unfortunate matter secret—that a young woman living with the liberty which is permitted to girls of your nation could not possibly be ignorant of the probable result of encouraging Don Vittorio's love-making in such a case. The world will say that Lucia *perhaps* played for the great prize of wife, but failing that, would not disdain to content herself with——'

'Be silent, sir ! This conversation is

worse than useless. I have nothing to say to you. I recognise no right on your part to intrude yourself into my private life. A benevolent intention might excuse it; but you are evidently actuated by feelings which are not benevolent.'

'Young woman, I am not accustomed to be so addressed.'

'Nor I.'

'I am fulfilling my duty——'

'If so, your duty and my duty clash. This is my house, Monsignore. I request you, as you are a gentleman, to leave it.'

'Before doing so, I wish to speak with your sister.'

'I shall oppose your seeing her. She is too much prostrated to be equal to such an interview.'

'Do you mean to shut her up? You

had better be careful about what you are doing !'

'Oh, sir, do not condescend to threaten me ! I am not to be terrified by stern looks and big words. I am ashamed to continue this scene ! Let it end. Since you refuse to go, I will leave you.'

No sooner said than done. I passed swiftly out of the room, along the corridor, and up the stairs which led to our bedroom, leaving Monsignore in a position of considerable discomfiture. As I went through the stone corridor, I fancied I saw something flitting on in front of me; and before I reached our bedroom door, I overtook Lucy, trembling and panting with the haste she had made.

'Lucy!' I cried, ' what does this mean ? Where have you been ? Why did you leave your bed ?'

She drew me into the room and shut the door before she answered, and then, sitting down on the side of the bed, she laid her head against my breast, and said, ' I fell asleep after you left me, and when I awoke my headache was gone. I felt better, calmer, less fevered and nervous, than I have felt since I read that letter. I wrapped a shawl round me and came down to the sitting-room to tell you this, and to give you one gleam of comfort in the midst of all the trouble I cause you. When I reached the door, I heard a voice speaking angrily. I did not recognise it at first, it was so changed. But after a few moments I found it was Monsignor Chiappaforti who was speaking. And then you answered him. And I stood there out of sight, and —and I heard it all, Catherine !'

CHAPTER XI.

THE RAW MATERIAL.

'But, Catty dear,' said my sister to me the next morning, when we were pacing slowly together, arm in arm, out of the sunshine into the shadow, and out of the shadow into the sunshine, in the gardens of the Villa d'Este, 'Catty dear, I cannot think that Vittorio meant to deceive me.'

Lucy was still pale and weak, with heavy circles round her pretty blue eyes, and her gown, which had fitted her so neatly two months ago, hanging loosely about her meagre form; but the blue eyes had a bright, steady look of resolution in them which was new, and her slender figure no longer drooped in the listless way which it had so pained me to see. We had talked and talked half the night through; and for the first time for many weeks I had felt that Lucy was speaking her whole mind, and her whole heart, which was better, to me. The veil through which we had been seeing each other dimly was gone. My own candid, simple-minded little Lucy had come back to me, and my heart was lightened of a load. The very half-soft, half-stubborn way she had of persisting in her own opinion about that poor creature, Vittorio Corleoni, re-minded me of the fair mite of a child, with a wide forehead and sensitive mouth, whom my brother used to call little Square-toes in her nursery days; declaring that her small shoes with straps to them (how small they were !) had a certain air of innocent obstinacy, which gave them a mysterious resemblance to their owner.

'Lucy,' said I, 'we will not discuss Don Vittorio unless you choose. But if we are to discuss him I must speak out my thoughts, must I not ?'

'Y—es, Catherine.' Then after a minute's pause she added more firmly, 'Yes. Speak out. It is best, although it may hurt a little for the moment. And, Catherine, I have been thinking and thinking, and trying to see things sincerely ; and one thing I have seen. And that is, that if what you say pains me, what I say may equally pain you !'

'True, Lucy. Fairly and honestly said.'

I was pleased to hear her say this—none the less pleased because I thought it augured worse for the influence over her of Monsignor

Chiappaforti, and the special advocates of
his Church, than any utterance from her
lips which I could recall.   And on this clear
and open footing we discussed together the
whole story of Don Vittorio's wooing from
the beginning, and of the Princess's singular
sweetness, followed by sudden severity, and
of Monsignore's part in the little drama.
The cool, easy, matter-of-course way in
which Monsignore had accepted it as certain
that Don Vittorio meant to deceive Lucy,
and betray her trust and love, had, I could
see, perilously shaken that dignitary's position in my sister's estimation, even if it had
not toppled him over altogether.   I well
knew that Monsignore would never have
spoken as he did speak had he known that
Lucy was within earshot.   He might, indeed, have expressed the same meaning, but
in a very, very different tone.   However, I

did not insist on this point, thinking it best to leave time, and reflection, and her own conscience to do their silent work in her mind. But she clung to her belief in Don Vittorio's truth and honour with a tenacity that made me sad. And yet I loved her for it.

'Why, Catherine, can I doubt him merely because others do ? I should be——' She paused, and the tears sprang to her eyes and her cheeks flushed ; but she bravely finished her sentence without a sob—'I should be as bad as the Princess thinks me, if I didn't believe in Vittorio with all my heart.'

'Ah, my child, don't nurse vain hopes and illusions !'

'As to hopes—no. I see now very clearly that we were both foolish. Who am I that he should stoop to marry me ? It was a foolish dream, and I see now that

it was selfish of me to think of—of being
his wife.   He ought to marry a lady of his
own rank, with riches and beauty, and all
good gifts far above mine.   And I—hope he
will.   But I don't want him to forget me
altogether.   I want him to think of me
always as wishing him well and happy, and
praying for God's blessing on him and his.
As for me, I shall never care for anyone
else—never, never.   But I dare say that
some day I shall be glad to think that I
didn't ruin his life and separate him from his
own people.   And he will get over this
trouble, and love someone else—as I never,
never can.   But then—men are different.
He won't be to blame, Catherine.'

The tears were streaming down her pale
cheeks now, but yet her face had a look of
serenity through it all.   It was better for
her to talk freely than to keep her innocent

sorrows to herself. 'And so, perhaps, Lucy may be spared the rude disenchantment which I feared for her ; and may be able to look back in future years, when she is a happy wife and mother, on this love-story with a pleasant tenderness, as one remembers the dreams of childhood.'

Thus ran my thoughts. For, you see, I paid very little heed to Lucy's protestations that she could never, never love anyone else. She believed it. But at her age, and with her character, that was as natural as that she should be mistaken in so believing.

'No,' said she, drying her eyes, as she stood with her face turned towards the great plain, with Rome rising from its misty horizon like a phantom city ; 'no, that is over for me. But human beings have different gifts and different missions, and perhaps too much earthly happiness may

clog the wings of the spirit, especially if it
is but a weak, faltering spirit like mine—
and some of us may need sorrow and disappointment to teach us the beauty and
value of a prayerful life.'

' Well,' I answered, '"*Laborare est orare*,"
you know, Lucy.   And I must not lose any
more of the daylight, but set to work on my
study of that gentle damsel, Monica.'

I cannot tell why—I have never been
able to account for the thought coming into
my head precisely then, and not sooner—
but the fact is, that scarcely had I uttered
the last words about Monica, when a sudden
idea—almost a conviction—rushed into my
mind in connection with her, and sent a hot,
startled flush over my face.   Lucy did not
see it, for she was still gazing out at the
view in an absent-minded way.   We left the
Villa d'Este, and returned to our lodgings

together. I thought my sister had had walking enough, and advised her to lie down and rest awhile whilst I worked. She declared that she was not tired, and that she wished to do something for me, who was always so industrious and ready to work under difficulties ; and she proposed to finish a piece of needlework that I had in hand. But when we had climbed up the dark, dirty stone staircase leading to our abode, she was obliged to own herself very weary, and to take my advice about lying down.

' I shall only lie still some half hour or so, Catherine,' she said, 'and then come and have a look at your study, if I may. I should like to see Monica again, too. I wonder what became of that poor girl—her brother's sweetheart, you know. Poor thing ! to be taken away from her home and her innocent country life, and the love of an honest man—and then deserted ! How sad it is to think of ! I have thought of that girl several times since you told me the story.'

It disturbed me greatly to hear her begin on this theme, after the idea which had flashed into my mind in the Villa d'Este ; and I had not been in presence of my model two minutes before she (Monica) said abruptly, staring at me loweringly with her great dark eyes, ' You never told me you knew him, when I was talking to you so free and open the other day.'

I knew as well what was coming as if I had had it printed clearly on a page before my eyes. But it was necessary to preserve my cool self-command with Monica, under penalty of forfeiting what little influence I had acquired over her. So I answered quietly, ' In the first place, draw that plait

more forward, and let it shade the throat—
so!' (I was pointing at the tresses of her
wonderful blue-black, coarse, thick hair.)
'And in the next place, speak clearly if you
want me to understand you.'

She had mechanically obeyed my injunc-
tions as to the disposition of her hair, but
continued to glare at me with an expression
like that of a buffalo-calf—if you have never
chanced to see one of those savage denizens
of the Campagna, I may tell you that the
habitual expression of a young buffalo is not
prepossessing, being at once sullen and dis-
trustful; whilst that of an old buffalo is in
general diabolic.

'Well,' resumed Monica, after a short
pause, 'if you don't know him your sister
does. I saw her on Wednesday coming out
of the gardens of the Villa d'Este, and I
said to someone I know—he wheels the

barrow to pick up the dead leaves in there
—"That's an English girl," said I, "her
with the hair like gold, and the face like the
Madonna in our church at home." And he
says, "Well, I should think I know that!
She comes here every day to walk, and she's
a grand Signora!" I laughed in his face,
and called him pumpkin-head, and I says,
"*She* a grand Signora? Go, you fool!
She's only a poor teacher, and her sister is
an artist who paints for money!" Grand
ladies never do anything for money—do
they?'

'H'm! I can't undertake to answer for
them, Monica.'

'Well, anyhow, you and your sister are
not grand ladies, are you?'

'Certainly not. As to that there can be
no manner of doubt.'

'Ha! I told Cecco so. But he's as

stubborn as our old black mule, and he stood
me out that she was a grand Signora because
the parish priest made so much fuss about
her, and took off his hat, and because a
grand Signore walked about in the gardens
with her, and rode away on a horse that
shone like a ripe chestnut. " What !" says
I; " a horse that shines like a chestnut ! Is
the man—maybe he's considered handsome,
with gold-brown hair on his face, and a gold
chain, and spurs that go clink, clink on the
stones ?"   And when Cecco said, " Yes, that
was the man," I asked his name—may the
fiend carry him away !—and Cecco told it
me, and then it all came back, like when
you wake up in the morning and remember
yesterday, and I knew that that accursed
Signore who sent Pasquale to the galleys
was Vittorio Corleoni.'

'Oh! Turn your head a little more to the right.'

'Well, but say, how did your sister come to know him? And why did you say nothing about knowing him when I spoke to you the other day? Are *you* a traitress, too? I thought you always said what was true.'

It must not be supposed that this estimate of my veracity was by any means wholly complimentary in Monica's opinion. She had never been taught to look on truthfulness as a virtue, and there might easily arise occasions on which truthfulness would appear to her in the light of mere imbecility, and lack of resource. Still, the fact that she had come to expect the truth from me as a matter of course, naturally strengthened my influence over her. And her ignorance and credulity, where she did believe, were as boundless as her power of attributing evil motives, and cherishing cunning suspicions, where she doubted.

'No, Monica, I am not a traitress, as you call it. But you forget that I did not know the name of the gentleman you had been talking of. I believe you did not know it yourself.'

'Ay! I had forgotten it. At least I had it in my mind somehow—hid away in the dark. His father has an estate over yonder,' jerking her head towards the south, 'where I come from. He goes there to shoot. He, that Vittorio—maledictions on his head!—don't go there now. He is afraid, perhaps!' Here Monica laughed, a fierce, scornful, tuneless laugh, and then, with a deep guttural 'Ah-h-h!' she spat on the floor, and made a contemptuous gesture with her quick brown hand.

'Come, come! Sit steady,' said I authoritatively.

'Madonna mine, when I think of that beast—— !'

'Don't think of him. You have thought of him enough. Think rather of some good person. It will be better for you.'

This idea, being a novel one, seemed to take hold of my young European savage, and kept her quiet for a time. I profited by the peaceful interval, and by the meditative expression of her face, always pathetic in repose, and worked away zealously.

'I don't know who to think of,' said Monica, after a while, looking up at me blankly.

'Sit still, at any rate! I have just begun to get the look I wanted!'

At this moment Lucy came into the room, and, standing behind my easel, softly

clapped her hands in approval. ' Oh, Catherine, how beautifully you are getting on !'
she cried. ' This head is the best thing you
have ever done !'

' Which would not be saying anything
stupendous in the way of praise, either !
Still, it is, of course, satisfactory to recognise
some progress ; and I think this study does
show some improvement. But this monkey
is the most tiresome of sitters. If she
would be quiet for one half-hour it would be
worth a hundred francs to me.'

' Let me talk to her, and try to keep her
amused. What sort of things do you find
to say to her ?'

' Well, our range of topics is not large.
Just now I advised her to think of some
good person, and I believe she tried ; but
apparently she never knew any good persons.'

'Who came into your mind, Monica, when you were trying to think of some good person?' added Lucy, in Italian.

Monica regarded her doubtfully, and shook her head. 'I suppose the saints are good,' she said; 'but I don't know them, and they live up in Paradise.'

'Who taught you about the saints, Monica?'

'Padre Bossi, our curate. He's dead. He was ever so old.'

'Well, *he* was good; was he not?'

'No. He used to beat the boys over the head when they laughed at Vespers.'

This was undoubtedly disconcerting. However, after a minute or two, Lucy, who had taken out her needlework, and seated herself in such a position as to attract Monica's head and throat into the right turn for my purpose, softly resumed:

' Is your mother alive, Monica ?'

' Mamma ? No ; mamma is dead. Daddy is dead, too. My grandmother is alive. She lives here in Tivoli.'

' Poor Monica ! My mother is dead, too !'

The girl fixed her eye contemplatively on Lucy.

' Was she pretty, your mamma ?' she said, after a short pause.

' Yes ; I believe she was. I do not remember her. I was a little baby when she died.'

' Ha ! I can remember *my* mamma. She was handsome, I can tell you. I am like her. I am a fine girl, you know, only the accursed fever has made me yellow in the face.'

I don't think any home-bred English person could believe with what absolute phlegmatic simplicity, and absence of blushing or bridling, Monica pronounced the dictum that she was a fine girl.

'Tell me about your mamma, Monica,' said Lucy, in her sweet, coaxing little voice.

At first Monica seemed unable to find anything to tell ; but a few skilful questions set her on the right track, and soon she was in a full flow of talk, recalling this and that circumstance of her childhood, with a plaintive, thoughtful look in her magnificent eyes (which look was chiefly the result of an effort to remember, and had nothing to do with soft emotion—but no matter ; it came out adorably on canvas), and a subdued tone in her harsh voice, caught by instinctive imitation from Lucy's.

'There,' said I, releasing the thumb of my left hand from its durance in the hole of the palette ; 'enough for this sitting. Lucy, I

am ever so much obliged to you. You
have been as potent over this untamed
young animal as Orpheus over the lions and
tigers. Isn't she like a panther? However, to-day I have really done a good
stroke of work.'

The sitting had been highly successful
and satisfactory to us all three. And
Monica inquired with much interest whether
the Signorina Lucia would be there next
time. 'Because,' said she confidentially to
me when Lucy had left the room, ' she
diverts me; and I like to look at her curls.
They are like the Gesù Bambino's, in
the manger, at Christmas. Have you
ever seen that? But, oh no! I forgot.
You are not Christians, you two. Some
foreigners are Christians, though; I've seen
them at Mass.'

' Look here, Monica : if you would like

14—2

to have the Signorina Lucia here at your
next sitting, you must promise me to be
good——'

'Oh, I'll be good! I'll swear if you like,
by——'

'No, no; I don't wish you to swear.
You must promise to be good; and you
must promise something else. You must
promise me faithfully not to speak to the
Signorina of Don Vittorio Corleoni.'

She broke out into a string of oaths
which would have been forcible in the mouth
of a carter, and ended by saying disdain-
fully, '*I* talk of him? I spit on him!
There!' and suiting the action vigorously
to the word.

'The worst of it is,' said I coolly, 'that
you *don't* spit on him, but on my floor. I
cannot allow that sort of thing in my
studio.'

I had often observed that Monica, despite her more than bucolic ruggedness and roughness, was, like most of her country people, vulnerable to sarcasm. Any approach to being ridiculed stung her severely, whenever she perceived it. So now she turned angry in a moment, contracting her black eyebrows, and looking at me with fierce, flashing eyes.

'Well,' I asked, as coolly as before; 'is it a bargain?'

'Why shall I not speak of that devilish beast to her?' returned Monica sullenly. Then, with a quick dart of suspicion, 'Ah, you like him! He is your friend, eh? I must say nothing against him, eh? Wait! You'll see if I care for him, or Don Gregorio, or any of them. Don Gregorio may take off his dirty old hat if he likes; as for me, I——'

'Not on my floor, Monica,' I said, very quietly, holding up at the same time a warning finger.

For an instant she looked undecided; but then, with another quick impulse, she began to laugh, showing her square, white teeth, and wiping her lips with her apron. Seeing her in this mood, I smiled too, and added, 'Come, I don't mind telling you this much: I dislike and despise Don Vittorio Corleoni as much as you can. He is no friend of mine, or of my sister's. His mother has behaved unkindly to her, and—frankly—I don't love any of the family. But, for reasons which you cannot understand, I will not have them talked of to my sister. If you don't choose to obey me, you must not come here. You know that I mean what I say.'

Monica had listened with an eager and a

brightening face. It delighted her to hear me say that I disliked the Corleonis. 'His mother, too, eh!' she said, nodding her head contemptuously. '*She* was unkind, was she? They are beasts all! An accursed family! And I hope the saints will send them all to perdition!'

With which pious and original invocation of the good offices of the saints, Monica threw a bright tartan shawl (my gift to her) over her peasant costume, and prepared to depart. But before she went away she gave the promise I had required of her, merely making the condition that I should allow her to ease her mind occasionally by talking of 'that accursed one' to *me*, whensoever the spirit should move her.

CHAPTER XII.

'A WORM I' THE BUD.'

My sister gradually recovered from the shock
of the Princess's letter. Nay, to say the
truth, she recovered from it more quickly
than I did. Her very humility helped her.
In the gentleness of her nature she bent like
a reed before the harsh wind; but, like a
reed, she rose again when it had passed. I
was less inflexible. I could neither submit
nor forget. My soul protested and cried
out against the treatment Lucy had received;
and even if it had not been in my character
to feel the injustice of this injury keenly, the

sight of Lucy's pale face would have been
sufficient to keep my indignation alive.
For although I have said she recovered
from the shock and prostration occasioned
by that cruel letter, yet she was very far
from being the sunny-tempered Lucy with
blush-rose cheeks whom I had brought from
England a year and a half ago.   Poor little
thing!   I began to fear that, for her, the
blossom and sweetness of youth had been
rudely destroyed.   That flower fades for us
all.   It is the doom of earthly things.
But for the happier sort of mortals it
changes naturally and imperceptibly, as the
fresh green of spring gives place to the gold
and russet of July and October in their
appointed seasons; and I had hoped that
my Lucy might be numbered among the
happier sort of mortals.   Certainly our
poverty and obscurity would not have

hindered her happiness, for she had been as cheerful as the day until lately. Poor little thing! Well, I could but work hard in the present, and hope in the future. Lucy was but eighteen, after all.

One or two days passed quietly. Don Gregorio did not come near us. And, indeed, I believe that I had frightened him nearly out of his wits; for when, one morning, I chanced to see him talking to a farmer in the street, he turned away, and darted off up a by-lane in a violent hurry, leaving his interlocutor gaping after him, utterly unable to discover what it was that had put the reverend gentleman to flight. Monsignor Chiappaforti, however, did not retire from the field and wash his hands of us after his somewhat stormy interview with me. He came again the very next day, but without asking to see either me or Lucy. He

merely left his card, with a polite message
of inquiry for the Signorina Lucia. Our
landlady, S'ora Nanna, was greatly impressed
by these attentions, and began, I think, to
consider us personages of some importance,
which up to that time she had evidently not
done, I am bound to say.

At length, one afternoon when I returned
from painting out of doors, I found Monsignore in our sitting-room with Lucy. He
saluted me courteously, and I could not help
admiring the tact and discrimination of his
behaviour towards us both. In general I
had thought his manner below his reputation
for talent; but upon this occasion Monsignore
was superior to his usual self from a histrionic
point of view. He adapted his face, his
voice, and his manner to the circumstances
of the case. It was the more clever, inasmuch as Nature had not fitted him for the

part of a feeling friend. Like one or two other persons conspicuous for jollity, and renowned for *bonhomie*, whom I have met with, Monsignor Chiappaforti's smiles and ready laughter always appeared to me to indicate an almost absolute moral isolation —a curious and painful want of sympathy. I know that he did not produce this impression on everyone. On the contrary, the world said how delightfully genial Monsignore was. But for my own part, rightly or wrongly, I found his uniform hilarity almost repulsive; and when Monsignore's infantine laugh raised answering smiles on every face around, it was an odd and unpleasant sensation to be conscious, as I was, of a dreary depression of spirits.

However, to-day he was serious, placid and friendly in his tone. I know not what he had been saying to Lucy before my arrival; but after I joined them he talked pleasantly enough, and avoided all subjects which might have aroused emotion. He talked of the places of interest in the neighbourhood, of Hadrian's Villa, of the Villa of Varus, and so forth. Perhaps his antiquarian lore was not profound; but it was certainly great in comparison with our ignorance. And, in spite of my dislike and distrust of the man, I found myself listening with interest to what he had to say. Among the excursions he recommended was one to Monte Gennaro—the Mons Lucretilis of Horace—and to the site of the poet's villa, near Licenza. On the subject of this latter Monsignore grew warm. He, for his part, was convinced that the ploughed field, under whose soil the peasant proprietor will show you a fragment of mosaic pavement, was the veritable site of Horace's Sabine farm.

Other archæologists differed from him here, it is needless to say, and differed from each other ; and every one of them irrefragably proved himself to be right (at least to his own satisfaction) by masses of quotations from all sorts of authors.

' Ah, I wish you could see the view from the top of Monte Gennaro, and then get down to the farm close to Licenza !' said Monsignore. ' A charming excursion ! You could go on ponies. I made it on foot when I was a schoolboy at Mondragone with my tutor, Don Anselmo—a very learned man, a great classical scholar, one of the *vieille roche* who belonged to the days when we *had* some learning and culture in Rome. We did not teach boys and girls out of the gutter music and algebra, to be sure ; but, then, *en revanche*, our professors had some erudition—could even speak and write their own language correctly, for example, incredible as the statement may appear to you nowadays!'

So Monsignore chatted on for some quarter of an hour, and when he took his leave I felt more charitably disposed towards him than I had ever done yet. I asked Lucy what he had been saying to her before I came in, and she answered with a serious look that he had been speaking of the consolations of religion.

The unexpected break-up of our relations with the Corleonis released us from the obligation of returning to Rome at the expiration of a fortnight, and I thought it would be well for us to prolong our stay at Tivoli for a few weeks. It was a great point with me to keep Lucy away from the associations of our Roman life, until she should be strong enough in mind and body

to bear the sight of the familiar places and
people without breaking down. I proposed to her, therefore, that we should
remain in Tivoli until the end of April, and
she acquiesced in the proposition with gentle
listlessness. Yes ; let it be as I pleased.
She would willingly remain. She wanted
to see my picture begun, but she supposed
I might work at it here as well as in Rome.
Of her own feelings or wishes not a word
did she say. This listlessness it was, in
truth, which made me anxious on her
account. It was so unnatural at her age,
and so foreign to her former warm-hearted,
eager way, that I could not help fearing it
indicated a morbid state of bodily weakness.
Almost rather would I have seen her give
way to passionate regrets, which would have
worn themselves out, than accept her sorrow
with this uncomplaining quietude.

There was only one thing which seemed
to arouse her interest and take her out of
her sad meditations; and that one thing,
strangely enough, was the company of my
model, Monica. Perhaps it was the fact
that Monica was utterly removed from parti-
cipation in the story of her life in Rome;
perhaps Lucy, in her kindness of heart,
wished to exercise a good influence over the
undisciplined creature; perhaps the mere
novelty and strangeness of Monica's un-
civilized sayings and doings really amused
her; in short, whatever were the cause, it is
certain that Lucy never looked and spoke so
like her old self as when she sat by, needlework in hand, whilst I painted from Monica,
and listening or talking to that wild
daughter of the Campagna. On her part,
Monica had some attachment for Lucy, in
her rough way, and a great admiration for

her delicate blonde beauty.　But she assumed a protecting air towards my sister which was very comic and curious.

'*Poveretta!*' she would exclaim.　'Poor little thing !　Just see her fingers sewing that handkerchief.　*How* small and fine they are—fine, fine !　And her curls are as soft——! just like the Gesù Bambino. Don't let her sew too much.　She'll be tired.'　Or else, 'Why does not the Signorina divert herself more ?　She never goes to hear the band play on Sundays.　She has no diversions—and she is so young !　You ought not to let her be so melancholy. *Mamma mia !* would *I* sit at home like that, and never enjoy a *festa ?*'

Once, by way of drawing her out, I said, ' Well, but how is it that you don't mind my being melancholy, as you call it, Monica ? I never go to hear the band play, either.'

She looked at me quickly, with her head on one side. '*Ah si! Per bacco*, that's true enough!' she replied, after a second's pause. 'And you're not old. How old are you?'

'Twenty-four.'

'E—e—e—eh! That's more than I thought. Still, it's not so *very* old. But —you ain't so pretty and fair as the Signorina Lucia. Her skin is like the wax angel in the *presepio* at Christmas, and her curls are as soft—just like the Gesù Bambino, as I always say. *Poveretta!* she ought to have some diversion.'

'Well, well, Monica,' I answered one day to a speech of this kind; 'she shall have some diversion. We will make a beautiful excursion to Monte Gennaro, and to Licenza. It will be lovely one of these fine spring days. And if you're good, and sit nicely

for me all this week, you may come, too.
You said you wanted to go to Licenza.'

'Yes,' answered Monica, 'so I do. I
want to see my aunt, granny's youngest
daughter, who lives there. Granny's too
old to go.   But—will that divert the
Signorina ?   Once I went to Licenza for my
cousin's wedding.   We had a tambourine,
and we danced.   That was famous!   But
—only just to go there in the daytime and
see all those big hills, and the river, and the
women washing on a work-day—h'm!   I
don't believe *that* will divert her!'

And Monica shook her head with a dis-
appointed air.   Still, the promised excursion
was something to look forward to, and she
was on her best behaviour for several days,
to induce me to let her go.

I should not have thought of attempting
it, except for the hope that we might have

Signor Sandro with us on the occasion. He had sent me one of his brief, hieroglyphical communications by post, informing me that he thought he should come over to Tivoli for a day or so, to look at my work, and get a breath of country air. If he would accompany us, I thought the excursion might be managed ; and for my own part I was very anxious to make it. Lucy showed little interest in the project, or, indeed, in any project or incident of our daily lives. She seemed to me to be like a person breathlessly waiting for an expected footstep, to whom all other sounds are merely disturbing. An eating suspense wore her spirit day by day. Once, when I said some word to her about the necessity of rousing her mind from vain regrets, she burst into tears and exclaimed : ' Oh, Catherine, if he would but come and speak to me, or write, or make one sign ! I know all is over between us. I am resigned to that ; I would never complain of it. But this blank silence is too dreadful. I imagine to myself a thousand painful things. What may he be thinking of me ? Who knows what he has been told ? There must be some mis-apprehension in his mind, or he would never leave me pining in neglect like this. He *couldn't* be so cruel, Catherine !'

What could I say to her ? To tell her that I believed Vittorio capable of almost any degree of cruel selfishness would not have mended matters ; on the other hand, to defend him was impossible to me. I could but assure her of my unchanging love, and hold her poor, curly, child-like head against my breast and let her cry.

Meanwhile I revolved in my own mind what I would say in my letter to the Princess. I was firmly determined that I would write to her, and now the idea that I might succeed in drawing forth some explicit statement of Don Vittorio's intentions spurred my purpose. Any certainty, however painful, would now be better for Lucy than her present state of agitating suspense, for under it lurked—I could not help seeing it—a wild hope, a vain trust, in Vittorio's vows. To me, his cowardly abandonment of her was as plain as if he had spoken it to me in the clearest words. But she could not see it as I saw. Could she have done so, she would have merited some part of the Princess's reproaches, instead of being the most trustful and unsuspecting of creatures.

END OF VOL. I.

www.ingramcontent.com/pod-product-compliance
Lightning Source LLC
Chambersburg PA
CBHW020111030726
47498CB00006B/2046